Lying on her bed breathing in and her fingers sore from the coat hanger digging into them, Vicki pulled and prayed that she was going to get the zip on her Pepe jeans up this time.

"Please Please" she begged to herself, promising to stop eating forever.
"You're going to end up with a chill, so you are, wearing them, they're not even dry right" came the mantra from her Mum, as she looked in on her lying there, straining with the coat hanger, half on and half off the bed.

Every Friday night was the same routine, Vicki found herself trying to squeeze into her favorite jeans because they hadn't been washed until that day and were still wet...well slightly damp, and that was the reason the zip wouldn't budge without the help of the coat hanger...so she told herself anyway, and every Friday night she was warned about this impending chill.

Vicki lived for Friday night to come with the

build-up beginning in school, where Carol and she would start planning their fun.

Vicki knew Carol from an early age, when they started school together and had become inseparable since. Vicki often wondered to herself why they had stuck together and were best friends because they were so unlike each other, but then she told herself, because of that they did get on.

As Vicki's fingers began stinging with the pressure of the coat hanger indentation, the zip finally gave way and started moving upwards.
"Thank God" she exclaimed aloud, rubbing her fingers, which had turned blue with the lack of blood.
"That you using the Lord's name in vain, AGAIN!" her Mum shouted down the hall
"Shut Up!" Vicki whispered under her breathe
"No I'm not!" she replied, as she got up off her bed and made her way towards the living room.
Sat in front of the TV watching "The Generation Game" were her Mum and two Brothers, John and James. Any other night

she would be sat along there with them enjoying watching their favorite TV shows and spending time together just the four of them. Vicki loved spending time with her family but Friday nights were what she and her friends lived for all week.

As Vicki entered John turned to look at her, " Where you off to? " he asked, "Out with Carol " she replied, glaring at him, praying he would keep his mouth shut and not ask anymore questions. She loved her Brothers but could quite easily choke them at times. Especially tonight because John knew what her and Carol got up to and was known to use it against her when he needed a favor. John was nearest in age to Vicki and there was only one year between them then three between her and James. John nodded his head at this reply and Vicki quickly went through to the kitchen, pretending to get a glass of water.

"Well Mum, can I??" She shouted through, not wanting to give John anymore chances of blowing her night for her...... " See you lot...I've not got much money, give me my purse through " Her Mum always said this but would still come through with a couple

of pound for her, so Vicki quickly retrieved the purse and took it through to her Mum, who was still engrossed in the TV.
"DON'T be late and watch yourself!" Mum said as she handed her £4... "Aww THANKS Mum, I won't "she replied nearly running out the door and down the path.

Carol sat at the dressing table, as George Michael was singing about "Careless Whispers "looking at her reflection in the mirror
"Where the bleeding Norah do I start..." she thought to herself, as she stared at the make-up bag in front of her. Carol had often sat and watched Tracy, her older Sister, as she applied her "war paint" as Tracy called it.

Tracy was five years older than her and everything Carol wanted to be.....
Tracy was beautiful and glamorous to Carol and her best friend Vicki and they couldn't wait to start acting like her, hoping they would both be as gorgeous and glamorous. Carol thought the world of her big sister and was proud when they were out

together because Tracy always had the latest fashions and people would always give her a second glance. The fact that Tracy was never without a Boyfriend just made looking like her all the more appealing.

"Think I'll start with this Pan stick..." Carol told herself, as she pulled the top of the sticky brown foundation and pushed it upwards, then evenly spotted it onto her face. Carol rubbed the foundation onto her skin and was happy with the outcome, as it covered her spots which had recently shown up.
"Carol... That's Vicki here! "Shouted her Mum from the hall.

Carol loved her Mum and Tracy with all her heart and even more so at the moment, as they had just moved into this little flat, because her Mum had finally left her Dad, after years of him hitting her and occasionally them too.
Life was hard but Carol knew it was going to get better now that it was just the three of them. The flat was small and she had to share a bedroom with Tracy, but it was better than living with the constant threat

of abuse living with her Dad.

Even though their old house was bigger and fancier she preferred the flat as it was quieter and her Mum had made the best of what she had and it was looking and feeling homely, but best of all she wasn't always waiting to hear shouting and her Mum being slapped or worse....and it was near her and Vicki's school.

"OK Mum....I'm still getting ready" she called back to her Mum, as Vicki entered her bedroom.

"Hiya...where did you get that?" Vicki asked pointing at the make-up bag and its contents.

"Tracy was going to throw it out and asked if I wanted to try it, so I thought we could put some on tonight" she said giggling, winking at Vicki.

Vicki laughed and lifted the Pan stick

"Is this that brown stuff you have on your face?" Carol nodded and Vicki began applying it to her own face. When it came to make-up and dressing fashionably Vicki was not as good at it as Carol, mainly because Carol had Tracey to help her pick clothes and she would often let Tracey practice doing make-up on her face, this gave Carol the upper-hand with all things to help attract the opposite sex. Vicki was in no rush to look older and if boys didn't like her the way she was then she wasn't interested in them anyway, at least that's what she told herself. They sat trying different colors of eyeshadows and lipsticks, giggling with excitement and feeling all grown up.

"Who do you think will be out tonight?" Asked Vicki as she admired herself in the mirror.

"Don't know" replied Carol," But I think it will be a right laugh "she winked at her best friend and they both knew what that meant.

CHAPTER TWO

During the day Lowe Park was a hive of dog walkers and Mums pushing prams chasing after excited youngsters. It was the largest park within the area and was home to a duck pond and two small streams ran through it encased with all varieties of trees and pretty flowers.

 Vicki spent a lot of her time sitting by the stream nearest the duck pond, enjoying the peace and quiet that she rarely found at home. Sitting alone soaking in the sights and scents of the lovely flowers and the noises of birds singing and the stream flowing gently by, Vicki would sit and day dream for hours about her future and what it might entail. This was her favorite place in the world and she often told anyone who would listen.

However, at night, it was a different place altogether. As the night fell it became a dark and creepy place to be, due to the wind whistling through the trees and the shadows from the night skies entwined with the shapes of the branches and Vicki's over active imagination, she always thought twice about entering the park at night...

Unless....she was with her friends.

"GO on now GO! Walk out the door...DON'T
turn around now COS you're NOT welcome
annnyyymooorrreee....." sang Vicki and
Carol as they walked through the park
gates, laughing and waving their arms
about signifying the words to all and
sundry.
"You know we're not bad singers" declared
Carol....smiling to her best friend
"Ano, we should go in for a competition"
replied Vicki, laughing at her own words.
"Well I s'pose this helps" Carol held up the
bottle of cheap cider and offered it to Vicki
who took a large gulp of it.
"Yeah, but I'm not sure if its ma hearing its
helping or ma beautiful voice "Vicki
answered laughing and falling over a
branch as they walked between the trees.

This had become their Friday night ritual
ever since they had turned 14 and they had
met with some people from school one
summer night, here in the park.
Now every Friday at school was spent
trying to plan their night and most

importantly, who would have enough money and who was going to get the goodies for the night... the goodies being as much cheap cider and cigarettes they could afford.

Vicki and Carol loved the excitement it brought on Fridays and liked the feeling of being part of something which they knew was wrong...but then everyone did it.

Tonight they had put their money (for chips) together and had enough for a bottle of cider and ten cigarettes. This was going to be a good night!

"HEY...Up here!"

Carol looked up the hill and could see a group of folk sitting around on the grass, "Come on" she grabbed hold of Vicki and pulled her upright then they both proceeded up the hill towards their "Gang".

Everyone was in high spirits, mainly due to the spirits they had/were consuming, and enjoying the night. After all there was the long weekend ahead to look forward to, as it was the weekend. As the night went by there was a lot of laughter and singing, always the same individuals providing the jokes and antics which made for a great fun time. Eventually as the night wore on came the usual pairing up with boy/girl. This made Vicki nervous and she hated the fact that the group camaraderie altered in the minutes before and after this happened because not everyone got paired or never got who they exactly wanted.

Jonjo McNeil was the biggest joker in the group and rarely paired off with anyone so at least Vicki had some company if she was left unpaired.
Vicki was always hesitant about being paired off with a boy as she wasn't as experienced as the others, who were slightly older, or even Carol. Carol had told her she had kissed boys and what it was like but still Vicki would rather not find out just yet.
Tonight as the rest of the group paired off and set off for home Vicki was surprised to find herself and Carol unpaired and stuck with Jonjo.....

"Well I s'pose they didn't like our makeup Pal..." joked Carol as she got up and helped Vicki to her feet,
"Nope better luck next week" laughed Vicki and linked arms with her best friend
"Who needs a boyfriend when we have

Jonjo.....HAHAHA!!?"
"Hey what are you two moaning about, I'm the pick of the bunch "replied Jonjo as he struggled to get to his feet....."Here Carol, grab his other arm, help the wee eejit up." said Vicki, as she bent to grab his other arm and help him to his feet.
Once up on his feet and walking between the two girls Jonjo began singing IRA songs at the top of his lungs......
"Here you better shut up or we'll end up throwing you down into that stream" threatened Vicki. They both knew what Jonjo was like with Celtic and Rangers, then there was his bigoted ideas regards "The Tims" and "The Proddies" as he called them.

Both girls knew Jonjo had been in a lot of trouble at school due to him fighting with the boys from the undominational school and did not want to end up in any trouble tonight. It was bad enough that they were where they were, been drinking and smoking without Jonjo causing them further grieve by drawing attention to themselves.........

Jonjo McNeil was the class clown, loved

making people laugh, only he did not have much to laugh about in his own life.....

Jonjo lived with his Dad in a run- down part of town. They only had each other after his Mum had died of cancer 2years previously and they were both still finding it extremely hard without her. Life before his Mum became ill was full of laughter and he loved spending time with her, sitting talking, laughing, telling each other stories. At weekends the three of them would regularly get in the car and Dad would drive them to either a beach or forest, where they would just enjoy being in the great outdoors seeking adventures. This was before his Mum got ill.....
Since then Jonjo's life changed beyond recognition and although he looked happy and was laughing and joking, inside he was extremely unhappy and struggling with living.

It was at this time Jonjo started going to St. Paul's Church just to keep him from going straight home from school, he found sanctuary within the walls with the stained glass windows and it was warm and he didn't need to explain why he was there to anyone.

One day he was sitting in the church
enjoying the peace and tranquility,
pondering his worries about his Mum's
passing and praying for a miracle to help
his' Dad and himself deal with their new
life better when Father Mulhern
approached him and asked if he would be
interested in becoming an Altar Boy. This
was a great opportunity and would enable
him more time out with his family home,
where the pressure was really affecting him
and his confidence.
Jonjo's Grandparents were over the moon
and his Dad was beaming with pride, as it
was a great privilege to be an Altar Boy,
and they all seen this as a real
accomplishment so strong was their faith
in Catholicism. Therefore Jonjo threw
himself into his new position, spending
more and more time within the church
walls. He looked up to Father Mulhern but
this was not unusual as most folk in the
parish did, but he felt he owed the Priest
for giving him this opportunity and helping
him cope better with his problems, as often
the Priest would listen to him and give him
advice.

The first time it happened to him Jonjo thought it had been his fault......

Mass had ended and the parishioners had vacated the church, the only people left were Father Mulhern and himself, ensuring all candles were out and all the sanctity items back in their rightful places. Once they had set the Altar, they made their way into the side room to de-robe and that was when it happened...

Jonjo was sitting on the bench reaching over for his trousers when he felt Father Mulhern's hand on his thigh......Jonjo' heart began racing with panic and fear but the Priest continued, rubbing his thigh slowly moving further and further until his fingers were inside Jonjo's boxers and feeling for his penis. Jonjo was frozen with fear and after the Priest had finished handling Jonjo, he kissed Jonjo passionately on the lips then got up and left the room without saying anything. That was the start and it had only got worse and more and more intimate as the weeks and months passed.
 That was over two years ago and Jonjo felt

he could take no more and had contemplated taking his own life, at least then it would stop and he would be with his Mum again.

It was a Saturday having finished serving an early mass when Jonjo cracked...Father Mulhern approached him in the hallway in the Manse and as he extended his arm to touch Jonjo's, he quickly turned and slapped the Priests hand so forcefully that his hand throbbed from the contact, Jonjo glared angrily at Father Mulhern and the Priest sensed there was trouble ahead.....

It was after this recent incident that Jonjo promised himself he was going to have to tell someone what Father Mulhern had been doing to him because he couldn't take anymore....
Jonjo's coping mechanism was to go out with his friends and try to forget about it by getting blind drunk as often as he could. At least when he was drunk he didn't have to think about anything but having fun and the hurting stopped, that was until tonight.....

Unbeknown to the three youngsters, someone was watching and listening, under the small archway at the bottom of the stream, amongst the dirt and undergrowth, was someone, with REVENGE on his mind and he knew he had to remain in the sanctuary of the archway in order for his plan to work...

CHAPTER THREE

Charlie Sweeney was the epitome of all the descriptives for a good looking guy...Tall Dark and Handsome.....some would even say he had a cool air about him. However, there was nothing cool about Charlie's temper which could quickly step up to a rage. He had an air of danger about him which a lot of women found attractive and alluring meaning he was never without a lover for long and this usually provided him with a roof over his head and food in his stomach. Charlie used his looks and weakness of females for his own purpose in getting by in this life. However, here in Hollowburn, he knew only of one person and in order to get what he came for had to sort this problem and keep a low profile. Charlie was 22yrs old and not from around these parts. He had come to get answers and find out the truth regards his parentage and revenge against the person responsible for him being the way he was.... which he felt was his for the taking!!!!

Whenever Charlie allowed his thoughts to go back in time he could feel the mix of emotions within him....The hurt, loss, rejection but above all else the feeling of complete and utter rage, soaring through every vein in his body.
All Charlie knew about his birth mother was that she had been unmarried and therefore could not have kept him when he

was born.

This was due to the fact she was of Roman Catholic religion and from a strict family which would never allowed the Mother and Baby to remain together because of the shame it would have brought on the family. So she faced the dilemma either being disowned and bringing her Son up on her own without help or support or bring her family into disrepute within the local community. Charlie felt she had made the wrong decision and taken the easy road out, which he certainly had not throughout his life and she would pay for her decision NOW!

"Ssshhhh" whispered Vicki, stopping dead in her tracks, "Did you hear that?" she asked Jonjo and Carol as she pulled them to a stop...

"Nope...nothing..." Carol whispered back, looking around nervously, she hated being here in the park at this time with all the shadows from the trees and it spooked her more so with Vicki imagining noises.

."Ssssssshhhhhh.....Seriously..., there's

someone or something over there " she pointed wearily in the direction of the archway at the stream, I swear I just saw someone, " Look! " she screeched, pointing towards the stream...The light from the lamppost was shining towards the archway and jutting out from underneath the archway Vicki was adamant she could see a figure staring back at her, she could almost feel someone was watching them.

"I don't hear or see anyone Vicks it your imagination.." spoke Carol becoming more nervous by the minute, " Let's just get out of here.... quick or we'll miss our bus ! " she instructed as she tugged on Vicki's sleeve, as she continued walking along the grass path.
Vicki gave into her friends demands and began walking downhill again, but as she gave the archway one more look back, she swore she saw someone and she thought she knew who.......

"Wow, that was a close one" thought the stranger under the archway.... he had nearly given himself away. OR had he...

He wasn't sure, but he did know he was

beginning to feel the rage build up inside him as he lay listening to the stupid young boy singing sectarian songs...this just brought out the hatred he felt for all things associated to the so called " Catholic " religion and the secrets he had discovered that they had tried to keep safe....
Given his association with the religion he doubted anyone could understand the deep resentment he felt towards it. After all he had been given sanctuary by the good old church....hadn't he!

"Tonight was a good laugh, wasn't it "? Stated Carol, " I couldn't stop laughing when that daft idiot Benny fell right over the hedge, did you see the state of his jeans, covered in dog shit, god help him when his Mother sees him....or rather smells him " the three of them laughed uncontrollably at the thought.
 It was guaranteed that at least one of the boys would usually do something stupid on a Friday night session (as it was called) Everyone looked forward to the get together and there was always the added excitement of getting a kiss and cuddle at the end of the night, if you were lucky. Tonight Jonjo, Vicki and Carol had not been lucky in that

sense but that had not stopped them from enjoying their night together.
They were still laughing about the things which had happened during the night as they reached the park gates with the main road ahead of them.

"You going to be ok here Jonjo ? " asked the girls as they reached the park gates.
 "Yeah, I'll be grand thanks for your company girls I'd have been lost without you..." Jonjo smirked as he made his way up the hill waving as he went his way and the girls walked down the road to catch the bus....all three glad to be going home....

As Jonjo walked he began humming the tune which had come to his mind, before he knew it he was singing aloud 'Fields of Athenry 'he was so lost in his singing and although the girls had asked him to stop singing the types of songs, he continued to do so, totally unaware of the danger lurking at the other side of the park fence.

Hunched up underneath the archway, the stranger could hear the three teenagers laughing, he watched as the two girls parted with the boy at the park gates and waited....

Listening as the boy began singing the stupid song, he should have listened to the girls and shut up singing, he became enfuelled by rage.

The stranger stepped out from underneath the archway, he could feel his fists tightening as he followed the youngster on the opposite side of the fence...

"Stupid idiot.... just stupid, that's what you are!" repeatedly going through his mind. Why would this boy be singing at the top of his lungs about something which meant him harm, it was stupid! He could see there was an opening in the fence, where it had been vandalised and was going to use this to his advantage.....

Jonjo, was away in his own wee world singing aloud quite happily when he approached the gap in the fence and felt someone grab him from the other side... pulling him over in between the trees and the dirt...

Jonjo froze at first then began kicking and punching his arms and legs as he tried to fight off his attacker.

The stranger's rage was at fever pitch and he was a lot bigger and stronger than Jonjo, he was uncontrollable as he kicked and punched Jonjo' shouting over and over " SHUT UP ! SHUT UP! "

Jonjo was trying to protect his body from the blows and pleading for this guy to stop but all his begging was falling on deaf ears.....
"Please...Please...I'll do anything, just please stop "begged Jonjo to no avail.

After what felt like a short time to the stranger his anger and strength were beginning to fail, the red mist which had taken over him cleared as he came to an abrupt stop....he could see the blood covered boy lying in front of him and slowly came to the realisation of what he had done...

He panicked as he saw his blood covered hands and clothes and was aware of an almost metallic smell, which he realized was the smell of blood.....
Jonjo's body lay lifeless covered not only in blood but dirt...the stranger pulled and tried moving to awaken Jonjo by shouting

to him "WAKE UP ! WAKE UP! ", however, the longer he shouted the more he realized the boy would never wake up again........

CHAPTER FOUR

"Vicki....Are you planning on moving from that bed today?" called her Mum from the living room down the hallway.

Vicki loved her bed and lying day dreaming but this morning something was annoying her....

Her mind kept going back to last night and although they had had a good laugh and she hadn't been caught drinking or smoking for another week, she felt uneasy.

Her Mum would kill her if she knew where she went and what she got up to but Vicki told herself it was normal and everyone done it, this eased the guilt she felt for going against her Mums wishes.
As Vicki lay convincing herself she had nothing to feel bad about she could hear the phone ringing in the living room and her Brother John answer it.....

" Vicki...it's for you " hollered John down the hall....Vicki sprang out of her bed grabbed her housecoat and ran to the phone, she loved getting calls as she wasn't allowed to use the phone much.

"Have you heard? Have you heard what's happened?" Carol was asking shakily and Vicki could tell from her tone of voice she wasn't going to like this news.
"No...What are you on about Carol? "She enquired,
"Its Jonjo McNeil....he's been found dead!!!" cried Carol down the line, Vicki felt her legs and hands go all shaky and she sat on the arm of the sofa.....
"Say that again.." she said , Carol repeated her statement only this time she included ,
" they think he's been battered to death

Vicki.." and Vicki began to cry
hysterically...........

The rest of the day went by in a blur for
Vicki as she tried to take in what had
happened to Jonjo. It was the fact he was
there last night larger than life, the usual,
for him and now...today he was gone...gone
for good and she would never see him
again, she could not get her head around
this fact, and pulled her duvet cover over
her head she began to cry again.

 Later that night Carol came round and the
two girl sat crying together and hugged
each other trying to comfort each other the
best they could. Vicki's Mum left them be
as she thought they were so upset because
they had known the boy from school, if
only she knew the truth.....She would kill
them both!!

"I just can't believe it Carol" sniffled Vicki,
"I mean he was fine when we left him..."
she was in shock and trying to make sense
of what had happened.

Carol sat upright on the bed..."Vicks remember you thought you saw and heard someone last night underneath the archway in the park...." she left the sentence hanging as neither girl wanted to think the unthinkable.

Vicki shook her head "I know but you and Jonjo never saw or heard anything." she was trying to justify not having seen or heard when she knew she had.......

Vicki had already had this conversation with herself once she had calmed down after hearing the news that morning. She had wondered if who she thought she saw last night had anything to do with Jonjo's murder, but surely not!

Vicki felt bad enough and was not wanting any attention brought upon her, if she were to give any information to the Police and then there was her and Carols parents...it would mean they would have to be told what they had been up to and Vicki couldn't put herself and her friend through that.

The days and weeks after Jonjo's death were the worst Carol and Vicki had ever endured....both girls had never lost anyone close to them before and were not ready for the outpouring of grieve which came from their friends and local community. Everyone was talking about the "murder " and trying to paint the picture of Jonjo's last few hours and there were plenty of variations to that, however only Carol, Vicki and their "gang " knew exactly what he had been up to yet no-one would tell......Especially Vicki !

It was a beautiful sunny day and Carol had persuaded Vicki to go to Lowe Park. Neither girl had been back since the night of Jonjo's murder, but they told themselves they couldn't avoid the place forever.

As they sat on the hillside looking down towards the stream Carol asked "Do you think you did see someone that night Vicks?" Vicki stared ahead at the archway of the stream and shook her head, but tears began falling down her cheeks...Carol moved closer so that she could put arm around her friend..

"It's ok Vicks I was only thinking...because, the Police don't seem to have anyone in their sights...do they?"

Vicki turned her head away from Carol and whispered under her breathe,

"If only they knew..." Carol pulled Vicki's face towards hers,

"What do you mean....If only they knew Vicks...If you DID see something then we need to tell them!" Carol was adamant now and Vicki was quietly wishing she hadn't said anything.

"Carol we can't tell and anyway I'm not even sure what I saw or who..."

"Yeah but even if you give the Police the information they can at least do something Vicki we need to think of poor Jonjo and whoever did it could do it again..." Carol was trying hard to make her friend see sense and talk, but felt as though she was banging her head against a brick wall, because she was getting nowhere with her....

"Carol..... If I did tell then our parents would know what we were up to... I don't want anymore upset"

"Yeah but isn't it better to tell and maybe

help catch Jonjo's killer than letting them get away with it or worse...doing it again ???" retorted Carol...

Although Carol was prodding Vicki for the information and telling her to speak to the Police, inside she wasn't sure she wanted to know the details or for her parents to find out what they had been doing that night, but she kept telling herself to be brave and think about what Jonjo had suffered.

"Right.....I'll tell you what I thought I saw and then you'll see it's not worth bothering anyone with...cos I'm certain no-one will believe me either..."
"How come...what you saying, " enquired Carol, curiosity getting the better of her. Vicki turned around to face Carol straight on because she would tell by her friends face if SHE believed her.....

" That night...I thought I saw Gerrard Donachy hiding under that archway" she pointed towards the stream and the archway, " SO now do you see why no-one would be interested in my tales and It's not worth the trouble we would get into off our parents.. "

Carol looked at her and Vicki could see the surprise on her face.....

"See even you're surprised...so there's no-way anyone would or could think him capable of such a horrendous crime...Could they?" Vicki stood up and put her hand out to help Carol up off the grass, as Carol pondered out loud,

"Well I don't know he's no Saint...Is he?"..........

CHAPTER FIVE

Vicki was right, the more Carol thought about what Vicki had said the more she was finding it hard to believe it was Gerrard Donachy she had seen under the archway.....

Gerrard Donachy was THE holiest person Carol knew apart from Father Mulhern, the local Priest. Carol didn't go to Mass and she wasn't quite sure what she believed, but, Gerrard Donachy was an Alter Boy and was never out of the Chapel...he was kind and gentle and came from a lovely home with strict Parents, who were also never out of the Chapel.....so she was having second thoughts about telling anyone what Vicki had said...

Vicki knew she should never had said anything to Carol....she could see in her friends face that she didn't believe a word she had told her. Vicki wasn't sure what was worse...the fact that Carol thought she was lying or that she was off her head.

In her mind Vicki had gone over and over what she had seen to the point where she was questioning herself. As often as she told herself it was him she lay thinking about the reality of this and then she would talk herself out of it again. This went on for an age...eventually Vicki got up found her shoes, put them on and grabbed her coat as she ran out the front door, shouting " I'll be back shortly " to anyone who was listening as her Mum and Brothers sat watching tv.

"Are you serious???" Carol shrieked at

Vicki as she took in what Vicki was proposing...

"You cannot think for one minute that this will work.." continued Carol, as she tried talking some sense into her friend, one molecule of sense would be better than nothing, given what Vicki was planning. Carol could see the danger in the plan in more ways than one and felt for sure that Vicki just was not thinking clearly or at all!!

"Vicki...there is soooooo much wrong with this and I don't think you are thinking clearly..." Carol was trying her gentle approach first hoping Vicki would agree and they could just let the professionals deal with this situation.

"Carol I know you think I'm mad but I don't see any other way to solve the mystery of whether it was him I saw that night or not... you need to believe in me! " stated Vicki, as she stared at Carol to the point she turned away from her...

"Vicki!! Even if it was him you saw...do you honestly think he's going to tell you the truth, because then he'll know you know and that will put us in danger...God Sake...he could kill us next cos' he knows we know !!"

Carol was almost shouting at Vicki and she could feel herself becoming more anxious as the moments passed, but this was serious stuff and she felt Vicki was playing at games, however , she would not allow her to play with their lives.

Vicki had come up with this "Great" idea of hers....
The plan being that her and Carol would confront Gerrard Donachy and ask him outright if he was hiding under the archway on the night Jonjo was killed...
What baffled Carol was the fact that Vicki did not see the danger in this...Firstly, it would come across as accusation, which could lead to all sorts of problems, including parents etc becoming involved, because Carol was certain he would run to tell his parents. Secondly (more importantly) if he was there then he would know they had seen him and whose saying what would happen then. MY GOD. He could bleeding well kill us, thought Carol.

Carol tried explaining all her concerns again to Vicki, this time ensuring that she emphasized the fact that once he knew he had been seen, therefore making them witness's they could be in more danger. Vicki sat listening to Carol, taking it all in, she wasn't stupid she had already thought of the problems but she could not see any other way around this and felt strongly that this was the right solution......

"Right the question is....Are you with me or not?" asked Vicki, resolutely as she felt they were just going round and around in circles...

"Well....I'm not going to let you go yourself, that's for sure...so I suppose I'm in...." stated Carol reluctantly, as she made her way towards the door with her friend.

St. Paul's Church sat at the end of a beautiful tree lined pathway and was the oldest Church in the area. It looked old and rustic with lovely stained glass windows with scenes from the rosary on them.

 Once inside the stained glass shone in a multitude of warm colors and even if you weren't "Holy" as Vicki would say, they still made your heart swoon with their grace and beauty. Vicki had spent many a time in this church, as she had been brought up

in the Catholic faith, however, as she got older, she realized she did not agree with all the teachings and more so the way she had been taught, constantly in and out of the church praying and singing hymns.
 Often on a Sunday or Saturday evening Carol and Vicki would tell their Parents they were "away to mass" only to go sit in the park or another friend's house until Mass was finished. Then they would go and take one of the pamphlets from the back of the church, which were always available at the end of mass, just to prove they had been. Vicki always amazed herself at the lengths they would go to, just to say they had attended, and this was also the reason Vicki felt she no longer wanted to be part of this faith, as she would often relate to its way as " brainwashing " and as Vicki matured she was very much her own person.

Carol felt the same but not as strongly as her friend, she was just more lazy and could not be bothered going. Both girls did feel guilty about deceiving their parents but felt that if they attended then the church and its "brainwashing" had won, so they were rebelling against the Catholic faith and all it stood for, this did not sit easy with either girl, which ironically, demonstrated in itself the strength of their belief in the faith.

As Vicki and Carol entered the church the smell of incense was overpowering, there must have been a mass on beforehand. This became more apparent when they saw on the Alter in his Alter Boy uniform, of white smock and red collar, Gerrard Donachy. At the sight of him Carol's heart began racing and she was sure it was echoing in the chapel for anyone to hear. Vicki's hands became sweaty and her heart to was also racing in her chest, probably from fear but more so she told herself it's just because I don't like being in here. The girls genuflected and sat in one of the rows of wooden benches,
"What are we going to do now?" whispered Carol, as they both sat staring at the Alter and Gerrard Donachy doing his part in ensuring all the candles were out.
"Emmmm...don't know..." Vicki was feeling less sure of her plan by the minute and was beginning to wish they had not come at all, but they were here now and she wanted this to be over...

"C'mon" Vicki whispered as she pointed towards the Alter, tiptoeing they both made their way to the front bench...

"Hmm excuse me...." said Vicki in her best "nice " voice Gerrard stopped what he was doing and turned to look at them..

"Hello...I'm not sure you know me...or her....but can we talk to you for a minute. Please?" asked Vicki sounding calm and feeling nothing like it.

Gerrard made his way over to the bench and it was then that Vicki felt for sure he had been the person she had seen "that" night...

He was shorter than she thought, but then again, he had been under the archway, Vicki could not stop herself from staring at him as he greeted them both pleasantly and sat next to Carol, facing them both.

" Hi...what do you want to talk to me about ?" he enquired nervously, Carol made a mental note of how well-spoken he was and felt for sure Vicki was wrong, just looking at the mannerisms of this boy told Carol there was no way he could murder anyone. He just oozed gentility and grace....

"I'm not sure how to say this. So I'm just going to come right out with it...Were you in Lowe Park?" Vicki's heartbeat was racing and she felt like she couldn't breathe properly, she was trying hard to hide both these facts, as she asked the question and more so as she waited on his reply...

"Lowe Park?" "When?" enquired Gerrard suspiciously,

" The night Jonjo McNeil was killed..." answered Vicki, looking him straight in the eye, no way was he going to get out of this, she would know he was telling lies when he answered,

"I haven't been in Lowe Park for ages. What are you saying? "Gerrard was puzzled by the questions, but was becoming angry as the insinuation dawned on him, Carol could see from his facial expression, what was going on in his head.

"Uh oh Vicki..." whispered Carol as she turned slightly hoping only Vicki would hear her. "This isn't good" Vicki gave her the nod of her head, but was still facing Gerrard, as she wanted to see with her own eyes if he was playing them.

Vicki looked him straight in the eye and asked "Were you near the archway? That's all we want to know..." her nerves were getting the better of her and could be heard in her voice as she spoke.

Gerrard stood up, in a clear and precise voice he stated " I have told you I have not been near that park for ages, I don't like what you are insinuating and in God's house....Please leave!" he instructed them both as he pointed to the exit...
Both girls got up and scurried out of the chapel, relieved that the conversation had ended but unsettled at the way they had been instructed to leave.

"Well.... That went well...NOT!" Carol stated sarcastically towards Vicki, who looked as though she were miles away.

 The two girls were walking towards Vicki's house, both feeling depleted and annoyed that the plan had not worked.

"Vicki, I hate to say it...but I told you he would never just come right out and tell you... EVEN if he was there" Carol knew she was playing with fire talking to Vicki like this, as she could see that Vicki was upset and annoyed, however, she also felt it had to be said. If only to bring her friend into the real world, she felt this needed left to the Police and we shouldn't be meddling in it.

CHAPTER SIX

Carol always liked Vicki's house. It was noisy and whenever she entered it she always felt at home, probably because she did spend alot of time there and stayed over... More so, recently due to her Parents separating and trying to keep out of the trouble in her own family life, Carol was seeking sanctuary here in Vicki's nice comfortable loving home, although Vicki would never describe it like that, but then again sometimes folks took things for granted and Carol definitely thought that Vicki did, especially her family and home life.

Carol loved her family especially her big Sister, but she was becoming more and more frustrated with her Mum and Dad.....

Carol just couldn't understand why her Mum had taken so long to leave her Dad, with him being abusive to her and drinking all the time, and now that she had WHY was she letting him stay over at their new flat. Their fresh start!!! It certainly was not the fresh start her Mum had promised her Sister and her because Carol was led to believe that their fresh start did not include their Dad. He was always there in the evenings and Carol knew in her heart it was only a matter of time before the heavy drinking and arguing began again, and her life would be up in the air yet again.....

That was why she loved it sooo much here at Vicki's because there was only her Mum and two Brothers, as her Dad had done a runner with someone from the pub years back. Vicki never really mentioned him, as she was quite young and doesn't really remember much about him, this Carol envied, she sometimes wished she couldn't remember all the fights and arguments she had witnessed and she associated with her Dad. Here the only arguing and fights were mostly between Vicki and her Brothers and Carol found these amusing not threatening.

"Muuuuuuum!" "Muuuuuuuum!" "John won't leave my room, tell him!" screamed Vicki as she pulled at Johns' jumper trying to remove him from her bedroom, where Carol and her had come for warmth and privacy. John laughed in her face and grabbed hold of the door handle refusing to be led out by his Sister....

"I swear to God to John...You betta move or else..." Vicki threatened him,
"Ohhhhhhh, using the Lords name in vain...tut tut girl, I'll be telling on you!" John was enjoying this and it showed...
"JOHN! Come here! "Called her Mum, John was still gripping the door handle and refusing to budge, when at last, using all her pent up anger and frustration from earlier, Vicki gave one strong yank of his jumper and he let go of the door handle....
"I was going anyway..." he niggled at her, Vicki just tutted loudly then banged the door closed behind him.
"Thank God for that "sighed Vicki, "He's a right royal pain getting..." she flew onto the bed next to Carol, who was laughing and secretly enjoying the show......

"Right...what do you think we should do now...?" Vicki asked staring at the ceiling and hoping for a bit of inspiration from somewhere......
Carol who was lying on top of Vicki's bed turned onto her side looking at her friend, feeling more hopeless about the situation than she ever had before,

"I honestly don't think he had anything to do with it Vicks, he just doesn't come across as the type to be lurking about in the dark...does he?" hoping this would be the last conversation they had about the murder. Carol felt it was becoming all-consuming and looked forward to the days they had fun again....

"He does come across quite nice... but that doesn't mean anything"

"Ano but I kind of believed him and Gerrard is serious about his faith and all that guff, so I don't think he would lie...'specially in Chapel..."

Carol felt as though she were clutching at straws, but was not going near Gerrard again, of that she was certain. Vicki sat up on the bed,

"Carol...just cos he's a flaming Alter Boy means nothing...he can't still lose the plot, he's human, you said it yourself"

"That was before I saw him "Carols voice becoming louder as she tried to get her point across.

"Did he look like the person you saw..? " asked Carol hoping this would help de-escalate the situation from exploding into a shouting match, which she was sure would

happen, so appease Vicki she
would...anything for peace and quiet.
"Yeah he does although he is shorter than I
thought but then again he was under an
archway..." Vicki was sure it had been
Gerrard that night Jonjo was murdered,
she'd put money on it and she was not
giving up...she knew what she saw and it
was Gerrard....

Unbeknown to the two girls outside the
bedroom with his ear to the door, he had
just been removed out from, John stood
mouth open wide with shock at what he
had just heard.......
John could not believe what the two girls
were involved in.
"How could she be soooo stupid?" he was
asking himself repeatedly.

 He had heard all about Jonjo McNeils
murder, of course he had, it was all
everyone was talking about even his mates.

The story was that he had been jumped
and battered to death but the Police still
had no-one to pin the murder on and there
had been plenty coppers asking questions
door to door and in school. How his Sister

had gotten herself involved in this and kept her mouth closed proved to him how much trouble she was in, cos Vicki couldn't keep a secret !

The question going around John's head now was what was he going to do with the information.......

CHAPTER SEVEN

Once he had finished his duties at St. Paul's Gerrard Donachy made straight for home. He was meant to be meeting some friends at the youth club run by the church, but after his visitors today Gerrard was in no mood for socialising and having fun. Gerrard was more concerned about what the two girls had insinuated with their questions and was wondering how he was even part of their equation into the murder of Jonjo McNeil.

 Gerrard headed straight to his bedroom and closed the door gently behind him, threw his schoolbag aside and leapt onto his bed and began to cry....
All he kept repeating to himself was the question "HOW?"
The thing which kept coming back to him was the fact that the girl Vicki, who he knew from church and school but had never really spoken to, seemed really adamant that he did have something to answer to. What troubled Gerrard was...What exactly?

Gerrard knew Jonjo through school and the Church, but the two boys were oceans apart and had nothing in common, Gerrard had never spoken to him on a personal basis, but he did know Jonjo was a character and popular with plenty of friends, whereas, he was more reserved and kept to his friends at the church.

"Gerrard??... Was that you coming in?"" enquired his Mother as she knocked gently on his bedroom door.

"Yes Mother, I have a sore head so I'm just going to go to sleep." he replied, hoping this would put her off entering" Just let me check you are ok and then I'll let you sleep Son " persisted his Mother, as she slowly entered his room,

"Don't put the light on Mother..." he did not want her to see his face because then she would know he had been crying and he didn't want to worry her.

As she came over in the direction of his bed Gerrard said softly, "Mother I'll be ok, I just need a sleep think I've been studying too much, that's all..." praying that would put her off coming any closer. His Mother stood and tried to see his face but Gerrard pulled his duvet up further...

"Ok Son I'll let you sleep but give me a shout if you need anything...OK"

"Yeah" he replied, closing his eyes and hoping she would just leave him alone. Eventually after what seemed like a lifetime his Mother left his room and closed the door over fully.

Gerrard could not imagine what his Parents reaction would be to the accusations of the two girls. Both his Parents were strict Catholics and even more strict where he was concerned. Gerrard had always tried to be the type of Son they wanted although sometimes he felt they pushed him too hard and felt the pressure of trying to be perfect, after all no-one was perfect but this was no excuse to his Parents....

The expectations from his Parents was the reason that he could NEVER tell them what Father Mulhern had been doing to him. He knew they would never believe him if he did try to explain what had been going on for past few months and he felt so dirty and hopeless.

Gerrard enjoyed helping out at the church and he did believe in God, although more recently he found himself questioning his faith and everything surrounding it... There were times when he wished he could be more like the popular boys at school and to be included in their fun and games, but, then he would think about his Mother and Father and knew he could not let them down.

Just as he was involved in Church life his Mother and Father were more involved if that was possible. They attended all the time, took to do with every aspect of the organization and Gerrard sometimes felt that they put it before him, as he struggled with the relationship between him and his parents, he wished he could just call them Mum and Dad, but he was brought up to call them Mother and Father which he felt was old fashioned and his friends would joke that they thought they were posh, which he got embarrassed about.

Gerrard felt that life as an only child was hard, mainly due to the pressure he felt came from his Mother and Father that he had to be the best at whatever he put his mind to. Sometimes he would sit in his room and ponder if it really was pressure from his parents or if he was the one placing himself under pressure of trying to appease them all of the time.
Life was not difficult by any means within their household. They enjoyed many happy family times together and the few boys

which he was close to often called him spoilt. This probably was true to an extent but Gerrard always had a feeling that just as he was always trying hard to please his parents they would over compensate in other ways with him. Sometimes he sensed that all was not as it seemed between his parents, certain ways they spoke to each other and would act when certain things were mentioned, he just couldn't quite put his finger on it.

There were times when he would catch his Mother staring out of the window and when he asked if she was ok or worried about anything she would deny anything was wrong and change the subject. Gerrard would just shake his head and put it down to his poor knowledge of the female sex.

OR..... maybe there was something which his Parents were keeping from him, as he would find his Mother daydreaming more than was normal and he just sensed there was a secret which he was not apart of.....

More and more he was aware of a tension between his Parents, he thought back into his younger years and felt certain it had been present then too, it was probably due to the fact he was a young man now and more astute that he was picking up on the vibes more.

He paid more attention to the interactions between his Parents, firstly out of curiosity, as he was maturing, he himself was curious as to the relationship between a man and a woman. Gerard was beginning to look at girls differently, in a more sexual manner and watched his Parents hoping to acquire skills in approaching and talking to them, however, the emotions he was witnessing, even he knew were not ones of a happy healthy relationship and this worried him......

Mary Donachy closed the door to her Sons bedroom quietly and walked down the hallway, all the time wondering what was wrong with him. Mary knew there was something wrong with Gerard as he very rarely went straight to his bedroom and call it Mothers intuition... she could feel it in her bones.

Mary doted on Gerard, he was her pride and joy and she loved him with all her heart, well almost all of her heart.....

There was a small piece of her heart which belonged elsewhere and it broke Mary up inside that she could never acknowledge this to anyone, apart from her Husband and herself, she found this soul destroying.

When Mary was 16yrs old she met and fell in love with Charlie Ballantyne and she was the happiest she had ever been in her life.
 Charlie was tall, dark and extremely handsome. He had swept Mary off her feet when they had met at the church dance and spent all their time together. Mary loved Charlie more than life itself and felt they were going to grow old together. Charlie and she would sit and talk for hours, listen to music and hold hands wherever they went. Mary had never met anyone like Charlie, he actually cared for her and listened to what she had to say, Mary felt valued for the first time in her life. It was a natural progression in their relationship when they eventually made

love to each other... For months they had gotten closer and the kissing and cuddling became more passionate.

Charlie had invited Mary up to his house one Friday evening as his Parents were going to be out and they would have the place to themselves, Mary understood exactly what this meant and was excited to be all alone with Charlie in his house, in his bedroom. That night was to change Mary's life forever........

Soon after their night of love making tragedy struck... Charlie was knocked down by a car and killed instantly. Mary was heartbroken and felt her life had no meaning as she had lost the love of her life and best friend all at once, she had never felt so alone in her young life.

Months passed and Mary struggled on a daily basis just existing rather than living her life....

One Sunday whilst getting ready to attend Church Mary noticed her dress and good coat were tight and pulling across her stomach and her breasts, sitting on the edge of her bed it dawned on Mary she had not had a period for a while and she panicked......

Mary had no-one to talk to as she had lost contact with many of her friends as a result of spending all her free time with Charlie and she knew there was no way she could hope for support from her parents. She had not one person she could turn to and she fell back onto her bed and cried hysterically.

Weeks passed by and Mary started wearing baggy clothing trying to hide the ever growing bump and was succeeding in fooling everyone around her but she could not fool herself much longer, she knew she had to do something and do it sooner rather than later.

There was only one person whom Mary knew she could talk to and they would have to keep her secret in confidence, the priest at St. Paul's.

After divulging her secret to Father Mulhern, Mary felt slightly relieved but more so scared, as she could see and hear the disappointment in him. Mary knew this was a sin she had committed in the eyes of God, but felt that God knew that her and Charlies love was everlasting and they would have gotten married and spent the rest of their lives together and happy. Therefore it was God who made this mistake by taking her Charlie and getting him knocked down, thus leaving her all alone like this......

Father Mulhern had only one solution...

Mary should and would have to go away to have the baby then put him/her up for adoption. He assured Mary this was in everyone's best interest and especially hers and the baby's, as she would get no support from her family or Charlies, who were still grieving for their Son, and she would be isolated further for having an illegitimate baby.
This broke Mary inside she could not think straight or see any way out of this predicament where she could keep her baby and provide for it and she thought Father Mulhern was making sense in what he was saying so she would have to go ahead with whatever he organized, as she had no other options and he was a Priest

after all, he was only helping her.......

Mary's Parents believed she was away helping another parish set up youth groups as organized by Father Mulhern, not for one minute did they question this as it would never cross their minds that their Priest could manipulate their daughters situation, as they were strong believers in the Catholic faith.

November 25th 1970 Mary gave birth to her Son, she called him after his Father and asked that he be allowed to keep his name once adopted.

Mary returned home an empty shell, not only had she lost the love of her life but their Son, the only piece of Charlie she had left, had been taken from her. Devastated, Mary went through the motions of living day to day, this turning into months then years, til the day she met Gerrard's Father.

Philip Donachy was a good man, genteel loving and caring and promised to look after Mary, even after she had divulged her secret to him, he told her he would always stand by her, no matter what.

Philip understood Mary and she took some comfort from this allowing herself to look to some kind of future.

Philip and Mary married after several months courting and a year later they were the proud Parents of their own baby boy, who they called Gerrard.
Mary was delighted at having the opportunity to be a real Mum and promised her Son she would always be there for him, never leave him and love him with all of her heart...well almost all of it...as there would always be a piece missing.

CHAPTER EIGHT

"JOHN CAREY!!!..." shouted Mr. Friel from the front of the class,

"Will you please pay attention boy!!!..." John startled, turned to face the Teacher, he had been miles away in his head wondering what he should do with his new found knowledge regarding, "that goody two shoes Gerrard Donachy "

John knew Gerrard from school and church and he did not like him one bit. The boy was always trying to make out he was something he was not and everyone thought the sun shone from his backside... Well John would be letting everyone know he was something...he was a Murderer!

John had thought of nothing else since overhearing Carol and Vicki talk about their "Secret" he knew he had to tell his Mum and the Police, BUT.... could come out of this a hero, he was thinking , before Mr. Friel brought him back to reality.

First, though John had come up with a plan to have some fun with Gerrard Donachy...keep him on his toes....even earn himself a bit of cash.

Gerrard did not want to go to school the days after the two girls had visited him with their terrible accusations, he thought everyone would be talking and pointing the finger at him the way in which they had. He was having problems concentrating in class and carrying out his duties in church on the Altar because he couldn't sleep. He kept thinking about the accusations from the girls and he was worried senseless. Gerrard just could not fathom out where such an accusation could have come from, as he had nothing at all to do with Jonjo's death, however, he felt he had to try and find out why the two girls had come to their conclusion about him.

More so his Mother was watching his every move as she could see he was struggling and this put more pressure on him as he hated upsetting her. He decided, he would confront both girls and try help them and hopefully himself in the process......

Passing his locker, on his way to his next

class, Gerrard saw a white piece of paper sticking out from the bottom of it. Curious, he approached and pulled it free, opening it he did not recognize the writing as he read,

"I KNOW WHAT YOU DID........
I know and will tell. UNLESS.....you leave £50 in the bin outside of the canteen at 9pm tonight....
YOU HAVE BEEN WARNED!!! "

The color drained from Gerrard's face and he felt faint. He slid down the wall next to the lockers still holding the piece of paper and felt drained with fear. Gerrard felt sick at the thought that someone knew what had been taking place in the vestry with Father Mulhern and panic and embarrassment had overtaken him.

Watching from along the corridor John Carey was trying to read his victims every move with interest. John was convinced he would be quid's in later that night......

Time passed and eventually Gerrard stood up and proceeded to the front doors exiting the school, all the while unaware that John Carey was the one blackmailing him, not for the reason he assumed, he passed him in the corridor as he left.

Gerard's mind was in over drive, "Who could be doing this to me ?" over and over in his mind, the more he thought it the faster he was walking and not looking where he was going, Gerrard walked at speed out the school gates and straight onto the main road and was struck by a lorry......his last thought was ,
"WHY ME?"

Hearing a commotion outside John ran to the front doors of the school building and panic rose in him immediately....

There outside the school gates he saw a lorry and beneath the lorry lying, not moving at all was Gerrard Donachy's lifeless body with blood oozing from his head and in his right hand a piece of white paper....

John ran to the front of the crowd which had appeared around the tragic scene and he could not take in what he was looking at...

He stood staring at Gerrard's body for what seemed ages before he felt someone place an arm around his shoulder and guide him away from the accident scene.

"Carol..., have you heard who it was? The person who got hit by the lorry"? Vicki could not believe what she had heard and wanted Carol to verify what she already knew to be true, since her own Brother had witnessed the scene of carnage.

"Ano I can't believe it Vicki, It's terrible, his poor Mum, he was an only child you know..." this was more a statement from Carol than a question,
"Yeah so my Mum was saying, it's a real tragedy and did you hear he had some kind of note in his hand blackmailing him...about Jonjo McNeil's murder"?
"NEVER!!!!" Vicki nearly dropped the phone, as Carol's voice shrieked down the line, a mixture of horror and fear.

Since finding out about Gerrard's accident Vicki was experiencing some mixed feelings she wasn't sure if she felt more relieved than sad when John had come home, looking as white as a sheet and told her everything....well not exactly everything... because he was too frightened to admit he was the one who had written the note found in Gerrard's hand at the scene of the accident......The note BLACKMAILING him!!!

"Listen we need to meet ASAP Carol, somethings going on and I'm not sure what..." Vicki was panicking and felt as though her heart was going to explode out of her chest she was so scared,' someone had written that blackmail note to Gerrard and they had to find out who because, as far as she was aware they were the only ones who knew.

John lay on his bed and cried silently into his pillow.....
He had ran to the front of the crowd at the accident scene saw the letter still in Gerrard's hand and knew there was no way he could get it back now. Soon it would be common knowledge that he was trying to blackmail Gerrard for money and now he realized the Police would want to talk to

him and ask him what he knew about Jonjo McNeil's murder.

  Punching the pillow with frustration John was quickly realizing he had just gotten himself in a whole lot of trouble through his own stupidity and greed, and not just 'him, there was Carol and Vicki too.

CHAPTER NINE

"Right Son....I'm going to ask you one more time...What do you know about the night Jonjo McNeil was murdered " ? John heard the frustration in the Detectives voice and knew time was running out, he was frightened and just wanted to be left alone, he had been here for ages and had not stopped crying.

He had his Mum sitting by his side, she had been allowed to stay with him because he was under 16yrs of age. This did nothing to calm and reassure him as he knew she would be angry and disappointed in his actions once he told the Officers what he had done.

The room they were sat in was tiny and smelt of disinfectant and stale cigarette smoke. There was the table they were sat at with four chairs around it and a taping device on top at the side.
 Across from John and his Mum sat the two Detectives who had arrived at his house earlier that morning asking him to come to the Police Station to help with their enquiries.

As time was passing after the accident with Gerrard, John was becoming more and more paranoid and this was affecting every aspect of his daily life. There was a big part of John which was telling him to come clean and admit to someone his part in the accident, but the bigger part of him was so scared of the consequences he just couldn't or should he ?
This was the constant battle going on within John's mind and he was fit for bursting with mixed emotions...

John had been in bed although he was not

asleep as he had been having difficulty sleeping since Gerrard's death. When the door had been knocked early that morning John knew before he heard the Police that his time had come.

As his Mum and he were placed in the Police car, Vicki stood watching from the living room window with James, that was when the tears began to fall down his cheeks.

Across town there were tears flowing too.........

Mary Donachy had not left her bed since she had buried her Son.

"Why had God let this happen to her again..?" this question was swirling around her head all day and all night. Mary could not understand why this had happened to her...first was the love of her life, Charlie killed by a car, and now her pride and joy, the reason she lived, her Gerrard killed by a lorry.

Both gone forever......

Leaving her heart broken with nothing to live for. Sure she still had Philip, who was also suffering, having lost his Son, who he adored, but for her this was the third big lose in her life and her second child she had lost and would never see or hold again. Mary was telling herself she was being punished and this was due to her giving her first Son up for adoption. She felt this was Gods way of paying her back for committing her sin..........

When he heard what had happened to Gerrard Donachy, he felt rooted to the spot......

Sure he felt bad for the Parents but he became more worried for his own safety when he discovered what the boy had been holding in his hand and the implications this had for him.

This being the second untimely tragic
death of one of his Alter boys, it was
beginning to worry him that maybe some of
his congregation could have put two and
two together and be trying to reveal his
dirty little secret ?

Someone was playing games and he
intended to find out exactly who!!!!

CHAPTER TEN

Philip hesitantly walked towards the door
to answer it yet again.
 Since the day he had lost his boy he felt as
though the whole of Hollowburn had been
through his front door.
He felt overwhelmed with the outpouring of
grief from friends and neighbors but
silently wished they would disappear and

give him a break to be on his own.

As he opened the door Philip was not
surprised to find Father Mulhern standing
there on his doorstep.
Ever since the tragedy the Priest had been
a constant support to Mary and himself,
fulfilling his role as their local Priest but
also as their friend and Gerrard's.

Standing waiting to enter the open doorway
he could feel his heart racing, he knew time
was running out on him finding any
evidence towards what was exactly in THAT
letter and he feared the worse for himself.
The only good thing was the fact that Mary
was still in bed totally grief stricken, for he
knew the moment she surfaced she would
be looking for answers into Gerrard's
death.

"Tea? " Philip asked, making his way into
the kitchen... "Yeah...that'd be good. How is
Mary doing today?" asked Father Mulhern,
trying to remain neutral in his tone of
voice...
"Still in bed, Father, the Doc visited today
and spent time talking with her, so we'll
just have to see..." Philip sounded exactly

the way he looked...a broken man...
Just as he was walking out of the kitchen
with the tea tray, they heard Marys'
footsteps on the stairs...

"Well...have you ever seen a dream
walking? It's good to see you Mary "said
the Priest, trying to lighten the atmosphere.
Mary gave them a gentle smile and walked
over to sit next to the Priest. Due to the
time she had spent in bed she was feeling a
little shaky but she was glad to see Father
Mulhern, as he had been a constant source
of comfort and guidance throughout her life
and always there for her in her time of
need.

Throughout the early days straight after
the accident, as she lay in bed totally grief
stricken Mary couldn't think, it was as
though her brain had shut down, to protect
her from the reality of the horror which had
befallen her again.

 As time passed Mary's thinking process
was becoming clearer, and she felt as
though a fog was lifting from her brain and
enabling her to see things a bit clearer.

"Why do I always lose the people I love"?

Was just one of the questions repeatedly going through her mind, there is only one conclusion she thought to herself, I'M JINXED!!

Day in day out whilst she lay alone in her bed Mary thought of her life past and present and everything she had endured and all that she had lost.
Unsurprisingly this was making her question her faith and she wondered what she had done to deserve all the horrible things which had happened to her and her family. Something had been niggling away in the back of her mind the more she thought back about Gerrard and his behavior, in the days and months before the accident....

The more she thought about it the more she was sure that something had been bothering her Son...

Today for some reason Mary felt stronger mentally than she had done for a long time and decided she would get up and find out exactly what had been bothering her boy.

She was a woman on a mission to find the answers to all the questions which were going round and around in her head, she felt this was necessary in order to allow Gerrard to rest in peace because she could feel he was not at peace and had not been for some time before his passing.

" Isn't that right Father..?" he heard Philip ask but he had no idea of the original conversation as his mind was racing and he felt overwhelming anxiety set upon him.

"What? Oh yes! Definitely" he replied and had no idea whatsoever he had agreed to...

"See Philip I told you so. Father will help us piece together Gerrard's last days, for he spent that much time in the Chapel with him....." stated Mary, with a renewed energy, and then proceeded to outline her plan to find out what was going on with her Son.

As he sat next to Mary on the sofa he knew this was going to be the start of his downfall....

"Oh my Lord....Oh my Lord "kept going over and over in his mind as he tried to hide his feelings and keep up the pretense of spiritual councilor.
He knew he had to get himself out of the situation as soon as he possibly could as he was having more difficulty than he could handle trying to control himself and the situation he found himself right in the middle of. He could feel the sweat run down his back from the anxiety.

This frightened him to the core as he was used to being the one in control.

CHAPTER ELEVEN

Life was carrying on as normal for Carol and Vicki, well as normal as it could be now that Carol's Mum had gone back to her drunken and abusive Dad.

Carol hated being back "home" and resented her Mum for being so weak and naïve in returning. The only thing that was keeping her sane and making life that bit better was her Sister, who she adored and was certain that she would always be there for her, giving her big hugs and reassuring her that things would be ok.

Oh and there was Vicki......
What would she do without her?

Vicki was the constant source of making Carol forget about her troubles for a time by having fun and keeping her up to date with her family's stories, which there were many and recently more involved her Brother John.

Johns involvement in Gerrard Docherty's death was still a hot topic of conversation around the area, many folk believe he was guilty in making the "accident" happen because it was his fault that Gerrard had run away into the road of the vehicle AND then there was the note which Gerrard had been holding onto, which John had admitted to the Police that he had written and put in his locker.

John was innocent in the fact that he had not pushed Gerrard onto the road at the time but he certainly was not one hundred percent blameless, as it was his fault that Gerrard had run and he had admitted to writing the blackmail note.

Carol would never in a million years say all this to Vicki because Vicki was her best friend and she did not want to hurt her or her family any more than they had suffered already due to the gossip in the town.

Vicki was super defensive about John although she could kill him for being so stupid, she knew deep in her heart that he hadn't meant for this awful thing to have happened to Gerrard.

The note which John had left in Gerrard's

locker that day had been scrutinized by the Police and in John's defense, he had no mention of Jonjo McNeil's murder in it, so this was his line of defense when faced with questions regarding it and Jonjos murder. John played daft well thought Vicki as she knew he must have over heard herself and Carol talking about it.....

The more Vicki thought about Jonjo's murder, Gerrard's accident and Johns stupidity the more she was developing a gut feeling that there was something she was missing about it all.

"Are you having a laugh Vicki"? Smirked Carol, "You have defo been watching too much flaming Nancy Drew..." she laughed...
"I'm serious Carol, There's defo something we are not seeing and I for one am going to find out WHAT! "came the reply...
Carol stopped laughing and could feel the dread start to rise up within her. She loved Vicki with all her heart, but hated her when she got a bee in her bonnet, because she knew that there would be no stopping her friend until she got to the bottom of

this.

 Carol realized the impact that all the carry on was having on Vicki and her family and felt obliged to help her friend as she knew Vicki would do the same for her...That's what friends are for...Right ?

At the same time she also realized the trouble they could be getting themselves involved in too and this scared her because there had been a murder after all and for all she moaned about her life and in particular , her home life and family, she had no desire to die anytime soon. Mulling this over in her mind as she made her way home, Carol thought "Well, in for a penny...in for a pound...." But still that feeling of dread was still there....

Over the next few days Vicki was busy writing down everything she knew about Jonjo's murder and Gerrard's accident, she always wanted to be a Journalist when she left school, as she was keen to gain knowledge and information about anyone. Other people called her nosey, but Vicki knew she had a flair for getting people to talk to her and thought this would be a good start for her.

Sitting on her bed she had found an old school jotter with a lot of pages left in it, this she decided would be her investigative notebook and proceeded to write down the facts, well facts as she knew them. As she thought back to Jonjo, she played the night in the park over and over in her mind.

Everything that he said, well as much as she could remember, the way he was, "well there was no change there " she thought, he was always the Joker, and the people who were there that night in the park.... "Mmmmmm......Maybe..." she thought to herself, as the idea to talk to some of the boys that were there that night, came to her mind. The more she thought about it, the more it made sense, so she decided that would be there starting post and jumped off her bed to phone Carol and fill her in.

Next day in school Vicki was feeling excited and eager to get to her Math's class as this

was the class where most of the "gang" met
and usually organized their Friday night,
as in who would try to get the alcohol and
cigarettes, everything needed for a great
fun night together.
  Carol and her, had been split up in this
class due to talking and carrying on too
much. The teacher had placed Carol right
in front of his desk, and Vicki was placed
right at the back.
Sitting at her desk up the back of the class
room, she wrote a note asking where they
were all meeting that night and suggested
the swing park area in the park, as she
planned to quiz the boys that evening and
thought she would have more chance
asking her questions if they were all
together contained in the same area,
quickly she nudged her partner next to her,
who in turn nudged hers and then on until
all concerned had seen it, this was
acknowledged by a small nod of the heads.

Friday night could not come quick enough
for Vicki.

  She had made a list of questions she

wanted to ask and had informed Carol that they would need to get there on time and they couldn't drink, as they had to make sure they got to the boys before they got too drunk. This went down like a lead balloon with Carol as she looked forward to her Friday night swally, because she could have a laugh and forget about her problems back home.

However, Carol decided that helping her friend was more important than getting drunk, just this once, as she hoped Vicki would get bored of the questioning and normal service would resume sooner rather than later, she hoped.

"Aye and hell will freeze over before I go near her..." came the voice of Mick Carrigan, sounding insulted, followed by jeers and laughter from the rest of the group.

"You know you want to...so just go for it ! " came a voice from behind Carol, she got a fright and turned to find another few boys from school who were more than drunk and falling about. Quickly she grabbed Vicki's arm and pulled her towards the boys she felt safer with, the ones they usually spent their Friday night with.

"Can you please hurry up and get on with your questions, it's not the same when your sober and everyone else is drinking Vicki...Get on with it ! " Carol was feeling slightly uneasy and did not want to be here and this was coming across clear to Vicki. "I'm trying Carol it's not easy trying to get sense out of this lot, hold your horses.." walking towards Mick, Vicki thought he might be her best bet as he was there the night in question and he was friends out with this group with Jonjo.

Walking over towards him Vicki managed to get his attention with a nod of her head towards the hedge at the back of the swings, to which he began making his way over to. As he approached Vicki she could smell the strong cider off his breathe and just prayed he wasn't going to take the mickey with her.

" You awright then Vicks ?" he asked as he sat down where she was standing, Vicki felt she should sit as well to get eye contact, she felt she would stand a much better chance of seeing if he was lying when she started asking him questions..

"Hi, Yeah I'm fine Mick but I was just want to ask you a few questions about Jonjo and that night he died... that awright with you"?, for some reason she suddenly didn't feel quite as sure of herself as she had earlier, but she reminded herself of the reason she was doing this. At the mention of Jonjos name Mick began to cry and this totally threw Vicki off her course, as this was the last thing she expected or needed.

"I know I should have told someone...anyone....but I just didn't know who I could trust or anything Vicks".....Seriously... I just didn't "Mick was getting more hysterical as Vicki tried to calm him down, there was snot dripping from his nose and his breathing becoming faster to the point she was beginning to panic herself, she stood up and shouted on Carol to come over quickly. Carol heard the urgency in her friend's voice and ran over.

When she saw Mick lying on the grass, snot and tears running down his face, "Oh no, here we go…Has he had too much to drink already"? she called to where Vicki was sat shaking her head, "What the hell…." Was all she could say, as she bent down she stroked Micks arm, "Hey Bud…what's all this about, Sure nothings worth this, Is it"?, the uncertainty in her voice she could not disguise, even if she wanted to, because she had a real bad feeling about this…

Vicki bent down next to her and they both looked at one another in total disbelief at the state Mick was in. "What in God's name have you said to him Vicki?"
" I swear to God Carol I only asked him if he remembered the night Jonjo was killed and he burst out crying " she replied, nodding towards Mick, who was still flat out on the grass although he had stopped crying hysterically and was quietly sobbing. "Mick I didn't mean to upset you like this." stated Vicki, as she began rubbing his back.
 "Ano that… It's just I feel that maybe I could have helped him.." he was stating in between sobs, he was still looking downwards at the grass, " I should've told someone, someone who could've stopped it

happening.." he continued, still facing the grass, giving no eye contact to the girls.

"But you couldn't have stopped it Mick, no-one knew it was going to happen or we wouldn't have let him go off up the road himself, sure we were the last ones to see him that night ", Carol was trying to ease his feelings of guilt because she knew Vicki and herself had already had feelings of guilt about that night and letting Jonjo go off himself.

"That's not what I mean Carol." slowly looking up from the ground," I'm talking about his secret...."

Vicki and Carol gave each other side glances, each ones heart racing, and each one dying to ask, " What Secret ? " but each one unsure as to whether they were ready to hear it..

After what felt like an eternity it was Vicki who asked, "What secret you on about Mick "? You can tell us and we'll try help you, you know that...don't you? " She was talking slowly and as calmly as she could manage, as she certainly didn't feel it. Looking her straight in the eye," Promise me…Promise me you two will help me, cos I don't know what to do.." he was starting to cry heavy again and Carol quickly sat beside him and took hold of his hand," Mick we promise to help, as much as we can "was all she could say, unaware of the horrors he was about to unfold onto them…..

"We need to tell someone about this, I mean an adult, someone who can help us." Carol was sitting on Vicki's bed with the covers pulled right up to her neck, she had felt really cold ever since Mick had divulged "the secret" to them earlier that night in the park.
Once he had told them about the abuse which Jonjo had suffered at the hands of Father Mulhern, and answered there questions about the who's, where, what's of the situation they had reassured him they would not tell any of the others but would try to help him find peace of mind for himself, they eventually had calmed him enough they were able to get him home safe and sound.

"I need to ask Carol, Do you really believe what he said, and I MEAN SERIOUSLY.?

It's a Priest we are talking about here…who's going to believe us."? Vicki asked with total disbelief in her voice. Both girls were shaken up by the revelation they had heard that night and were not sure what to do with the information. " I know it's weird, but these things do happen Vicki…what if he killed Jonjo because he felt Jonjo was going to tell on him.." they both stared at each other, a million thoughts going through their minds , "OMG !!!…" squealed Vicki, "What if Jonjo wasn't the only one he was doing this to?" "OMG! Don't even say that Vicki, that's not right. Is it…do you think he was doing it to ALL the Alter Boys?"

 Carol moved the cover down slightly as she was beginning to feel too hot now, sweating at the thought of the enormity of the situation they found themselves right in the middle of….

"I don't know but if he was doing it to Jonjo, who's to say he wasn't doing it to more of the boys…." Vicki gave the idea time to form in Carols mind and her own,

 "One things for sure….we need to find out! "Came the dreaded words from her friends lips and Carol knew this was just the beginning………….

CHAPTER TWELVE

" I think that's a crazy idea Vicki, seriously, no way am I approaching that poor woman or her husband.." of all the crazy schemes and ideas that Vicki had in the past this had to be one of the worst and Carol felt adamant that she was under no circumstance getting involved in this one...

The thought of going anywhere near Gerrard Donachys parents was not up there with her brightest ideas or schemes and she has plenty them, but this time she was on her own and Carol had no qualms about pointing this out to her friend.
" That poor couple are still grieving for their Son, the same Son you thought was guilty of killing Jonjo McNeil if you recall, and now you want to go ask if they thought he was getting abused and could've killed

HIMSELF !!! Have you lost the flaming plot Vicki"? She screamed down the phone line.

 It was a good job none of her family were in although Carol was oblivious to her surroundings at this moment she wasn't caring who heard, she was so frustrated at her friends suggestion. On the other end of the phone line Vicki was beginning to regret getting involved in Jonjo's secret and her promise she had made to Mick, although she felt Carol should take some responsibility as she had made the same promise to Mick.
 They were both out of their depth with this, the problem being, they had no idea where or who to turn to for help, as she was sure they would be shooed away as a pair of teenage girls with overactive imaginations.

The idea to talk with Gerrard's Parents had come to her whilst lying in her bed trying to get to sleep. As usual her mind was working overtime and she kept thinking how she could get everyone out of the predicament they were all in, Mick, Carol herself and even her Brother John, because if they could find the killer, then people would believe John and she wanted to help him and restore some kind of normalcy back in her once happy home.

Since the day John had been dragged by the Police from his bed, her Mum was so stressed and upset by his actions and all the talking which was going on behind her back by neighbors and folks she thought were friends. Vicki watched her Mum become more withdrawn with each passing day and she hardly left the house, for fear of the gossip.

The house, which used to be noisy and busy, had become a lot quieter as they were all trying their best not to cause their Mum any unnecessary anguish, although it was only now Vicki realized how much she actually missed all the arguing and fighting with her brothers and often found herself wishing they would happen again soon because it just wasn't feeling like her home and she wondered if it ever would again. This was the reason she HAD to find a way to solve this and she thought Carol would be THE one person to understand where she was coming from, giving the fact she was meant to be her best friend and had always loved coming to her house for the atmosphere which no longer was there...why couldn't she understand and see what she was trying to do.

"John.....If I tell you something....will you promise me that you'll keep it to yourself and help me...and, it'll help you too ,but you must not say a word to anyone...right " ? Vicki had found herself left with no other choice but to ask John for his help as she felt she was not going to get any more from Carol.

Since her last conversation with her friend, she had not heard from her and she felt let down by Carol's lack of support because she really felt she was on to something and the fact it could help other people not to mention her own Brother was annoying her. Vicki had always been there for Carol. She had listened to all her problems and every little moan she had about her home life and every other aspect of her life...but now Vicki needed a little support Carol was nowhere to be seen. Vicki could feel the anger and frustration build up inside of her and had come up with another way of finding out what was really going on with Jonjo's murder and Gerrard's accident and she was more adamant than ever that Father Mulhern did have a role to play in all of this.

That was why she had pulled John inside her bedroom as he was making his way up the hall.......

"Well, what do you say..?" she reiterated the question as John just stood there looking at her with a puzzled look on his face. "I need to know if you're in or out before I can explain any further John.." she was desperate for his help as she was beginning to feel alone and bits of self-doubt were starting to crawl into her mind about whether Carol was right and this should be left alone or to the Police to solve, but there was her gut instinct telling her she WAS right and she should keep at it. John's hesitancy was making her more nervous...

"WELL"?? she raised her voice and quickly lowered it again..."What are you waiting for"? She asked, more patiently than she felt.

"I don't know Vicki, this is all sounding a bit too serious for my liking, I need to stay out of trouble, I canny get into any more trouble, and Mum will kill me. NOT to mention the Police! "

"I know, BUT. . .What if this could help you get out of trouble John, come on...just say you'll help me...PLEASE " she had to add the please as she felt he was going to walk out the bedroom, then where would that leave her.....

"Okay...I'm in! ....this better be good Vicki and it BETTER get me out of bother NOT into more...RIGHT!! "

"I PROMISE John! This could put an end to everything and we can go back to the way it was before...PROMISE! "She adamantly stated, however, underneath Vicki was praying she was doing the right thing, only time could tell now...

"You mean to say YOU think that Father Mulhern has got something to do with all this AND you believe what that numbskull Mick told you? Are you off your head "? John was sitting on her bed shaking his head in disbelieve at what she had divulged

to him about her investigation so far.
 The way he was acting just confirmed to
her that she needed to collect as much
information and proof in order to be taken
seriously by anyone else. Sitting in front of
John, her stomach felt as though it had
dropped to the floor, "John If I can't get you
to believe me... HOW, in God's name am I
going to get taken seriously by other folks?"
She heard the pleading in her own voice
and John could hear it as well as see the
frustration in his Sisters face.....
" I'm not saying I don't believe you, I'm just
finding this all hard to take on board
Sis...Of course I'll help you...Right from the
start.....tell me again...." he said as he lay
back on the bed listening to his Sisters
story of events.

After what felt like an eternity, Vicki
finished filling him in with her findings and
feelings about everything, he had to admit,
now that he had got over the initial shock
of the findings, he could understand how
and why she had come the conclusions
which she had. This frightened him as he
came to terms with the enormity of the
situation but it also excited and elated him
as he realized he would be in the clear as

far causing Gerrard's death, well to an extent!

"Where do we start then Vicki ? " he asked getting up from her bed, he felt eager to help now he understood what she was thinking and the implications for himself could only benefit him in the long run, hopefully ease things for the family especially his Mum too.

Vicki was feeling relief now that she had John onside, she knew this was dangerous territory she was stepping into but she could not shake her gut instinct which was shouting to her that she was onto something special here.

If only she had her best friend on her side as well, she would feel better. There had to be a way of getting Carol onside as well, she would give her one more try hopefully she would join her and John as she felt between the three of them they would soon get to the truth.

The next day Vicki went around to Carol's house.

As she stood on the doorstep she rang the bell again and knocked on the door. It wasn't like one of them not to answer and she was sure she had seen someone move in the hallway just before she had rang the bell the first time

"Carol...Carol." she shouted through the letter box, she was beginning to get worried, "Carol...It's me...Vicki...." Just as she was about to give up and walk away from the door, it opened slightly and Carol pulled her inside?
"What in the name......" she never got to finish her statement as Carol rushed her along the hallway into her bedroom.

Standing there with her eyes red raw from what looked like hours if not days of crying was her best friend in desperate need of a cuddle and that's exactly what she did.

Flinging her arms around Carol she shushed her as Carol began sobbing uncontrollably again, "Sshhhhhh....it's alright Carol....calm down, calm down...tell me what's up " she was saying calmly, guiding Carol over towards her bed to sit her down. Once she had her seated Vicki sat next to Carol with her arm still around her shoulders for support as she felt as if she let go of her friend she would collapse, she looked so frail and upset, Vicki began to wonder what was going on, surely this was nothing to do the fact that they had not spoken for a few days.....

As Carol sobs began to slowly subside, Vicki continued to cuddle into her as she sat beside her,

" What's wrong Carol "? She asked quietly, "You know you can talk to me..." she was trying to reassure her friend. Carol turned slowly and bit her bottom lip trying to stop herself from crying again, "Oh Vicki...it's been horrible, really horrible." she couldn't help herself as she felt the tears start to fall from her eyes once more.
"What has"? What's going on Carol, you're scaring me now," Vicki pulled her arm away so that she could look Carol straight in the eyes.....She didn't like what she saw and she wasn't sure she wanted to hear why her friend was so upset...

"Vicki, he nearly killed my Mum, she's in the hospital and they're not sure if she'll pull through or not..." she was hysterical now...knowing that her Mum was fighting for her life was one thing, but this was the first time she had spoken the words and it made it feel real which terrified her.

"Who has..? " Vicki was sure she already knew the answer to this question but asked anyway...

." HIM!" she spat the word out, "My Dad... it was terrible Vicki. He had been out all day Saturday drinking, Mum was angry because they were meant to be going out later that night to a dance in the hall , my Mums friend was holding it for charity, Mum was really looking forward to it because they hadn't been out together for ages...BUT NO !! HE has to spoil it for her AGAIN!! "

"Calm down Carol...it'll be ok." Vicki had a feeling she knew where this was going but even she was shocked at the brutality her friend's family had endured at the hands of this man, especially her poor Mum.

"He would not take no for an answer when Mum refused to go out with him... but honestly he was in such a state he could barely stand upright Vicki…anyway he kept on at her over and over but she would not give into him, that's when he ran at her and grabbed her hair…He started banging her head off the living room wall…it was terrible Vicki, I jumped on his back but he swung me off and kicked me in the ribs…I've broken two…." She was shaking now and could see the tears rolling down Vicki's cheeks she continued, "I managed to get back up from the floor and call the Police but when I came back into the living room Mum was just lying, she wasn't moving…."

She couldn't say anymore, it was too hard. Vicki could see that Carol was struggling to tell her anymore, she reached out, took her hand and they both sat and cried 'til Vicki asked, "

And your Mum ?" dreading the reply……

Carol shook her head and looked straight into her eyes, "Mums fighting for her life in hospital, everyone's there just now but I can't stand it, just standing there watching her …they just keep saying time will tell…what the hell is that supposed to mean ?" Carol was getting angrier, "I mean one minute he can barely stand upright the

next he's doing that...I don't get it "!
"Rage Carol, that's how, the only thing is that now your Mum will defo leave him, he's done....she will pull through this Carol she'll be back to her usual only this time It'll be better because he won't be near any of you " !

Praying that she was right, Vicki pulled Carol into her arms and cuddled her as her friend cried and cried.

Having sat with Carol until late evening and her sister had returned from the hospital, Vicki said her goodbyes and made her way home.
Walking back home she could not believe that her friends Dad could act so bad hurting them the way he had, she hoped Carols Mum would never let him near them ever again.

Carols sister had come home from the hospital with some encouraging news, her Mum was off the ventilators and things were looking more optimistic for her, her Dad was in the jail, where they expected him to be for a long time, so hopefully things would get better quickly for Carol and her family.

Things like this sure put life into perspective she was thinking.....
And reaffirmed her desire to see bad and dangerous people put away, she would give Carol a few days but she thought this could help Carol focus all her anger on something other than her Dad and maybe be a good release for her to.

CHAPTER THIRTEEN

Vicki was right about Carol wanting to join John and herself.

Once her Mum was out of danger and recuperating well she felt it would do her good to focus on other things, although she was not sure about Vicki's decision to involve John was her brightest given what had happened before, when he had found out information regards Jonjo's death, but she understood her reasons why she felt she had no-one else to turn to.

As the three of them sat in Vicki's bedroom the main topic of conversation was where their next move should be. It was agreed that John would be able to get more information from Alter Boys, given that he knew some of the boys and he's a male, him asking questions about what it was like, what their roles involved being one etc, would not look as conspicuous, as if it were the two girls asking.

It was also agreed that Carol and Vicki would keep an eye on Father Mulhern as he was their suspect at the moment.

" So, if you start asking about John that'll be great, kid on you're actually thinking about becoming one yourself " instructed Carol, as Vicki started laughing,
" What's so funny ? , share the joke ...." John asked her, "I'm sorry I was just thinking YOU...an Alter boy..." she remarked, "I'm only joking...." She quickly added, as she could see his face start to flush with anger at her mocking him.
 John was taking his role seriously and this surprised her and she reminded herself how grateful she should be to him for helping her and more importantly believing in her.

"Right, I'm off Carol, before I start on her." he pointed at Vicki and walked out of the bedroom, "Okay John... Good Luck, take care...meet here at 7pm ok "replied Carol.

"Vicki stop winding him up! We need John to help get info from the boys, lay off him." Vicki was surprised at her friends turn around towards Johns involvement, as she had made her feelings perfectly clear on how daft he could be, but even she could see that her Brother would come in more than handy.

"Come on then, let's get our Detective hats on, Watch out Father Mulhern, here we come!" stated Vicki as she grabbed her coat from the chair and left her bedroom with Carol following her.

Mary Donachy could not shake the feeling she had.......

It had come to her a few weeks previous during a discussion she was having with him ......
She was certain it was a slip of the tongue at first but the more she thought about it, the more she assured herself it wasn't something someone of his standing should be having thoughts about, never mind voicing them, this was why she was convinced it should not have been spoken, specially by a Priest.

Mary had been complaining about the cleanliness of the Vestry ,the robe room where the Altar Boys changed, " It's not right Father surely you could have a word with them, I realize that I do the cleaning now and again, but surely these boys can keep on top of it."

"Oh yes I like it when they are clean and stay on top of it...." He stopped quickly, with a smirk on his face.

It was the way in which he had said it, it sounded seedy to Mary and his face had reddened slightly, or was she imagining the whole thing. This was why she had not discussed this with her husband....She felt sure he would laugh in her face as he would think it outrageous....but was it ???

This had played over and over in her mind and she felt she should trust her gut instincts, she would speak to Father Mulhern directly as she felt there was nothing to hide and it was her mind playing tricks on her or was it! Mary decided to voice her concerns later that day once she had finished arranging the chapel flowers.

It had been over six weeks since he had killed.

He had taken sanctuary in a small run down bedsit in the center of town, he thought this would be the best place to be, as no-one knew him and he could keep up with any news regards the killing. He was right, he had heard other people talking about the young boy's death and had learned more about his victim and his life. The fact the boy was Motherless as he had discovered she had died, had allowed him to feel some empathy towards Jonjo but this was where it ended.

Every time he thought of that night and what the stupid boy was singing and shouting he felt a rage build up inside him, so great was his hatred for all things Catholic. The stupid idiot deserved what had happened to him...the fact that he was singing about being a "Tim" and how great they were, showed to Charlie just how thick the boy really was, because as he knew, the Church could not be trusted!
The fact that he was in this predicament was wholly down to the Catholic Church, one way or another, and the hatred and disgust he felt strongly for the charade in

which it hid behind had enabled him to kill !

 He was intrigued as to the events which had followed the death. The boy who had been an Altar Boy running out in front of a lorry, sounded bizarre but then again he was one of them.. SO, who really cared, he sure didn't!

Nights lying in the damp and smelly box, he called his room, his mind mulled over his life ...Motherless...he would try anything to find out the true identity of her, the one person who shared a heartbeat with him. These thoughts only left him angry and wanting revenge for the life and love he had been denied.
Today, he walked with purpose towards St Paul's Church, he intended to find out what this Priest knew of his biological Mother,
"I can't hide anymore...I need answers I think I've waited long enough." were the thoughts going through Charlie's mind as he made his way towards the Chapel.
 He had decided last night that he could not wait any longer and why should he wait, he wanted to know his Mother and he

wanted answers to the million and one questions in his mind but one in particular, WHY ? Why did she not want him?

He had kept to his side of the bargain so now it was time that the Priest kept to his....

When he started asking questions after his adopted parents had told him of his start in life, he had been shown some paperwork, and one name had stood out because it was beneath HER name....Father Patrick Mulhern.

Years of searching and asking more questions had brought him to this place weeks previously. This was the day he had been waiting for, the day he would get the answers to his questions!

CHAPTER FOURTEEN

Mary stood before the Alter admiring her handy work with the floral arrangements which adorned either side and smiled. This was something at which she had a flair for, she enjoyed arranging the bright colors and taking in the sweet smelling perfumes of the flowers into an eye catching work of art for all the parishioners to enjoy when the visited the Church.

It was on days like today when it was only herself and the Lord in the Church when she felt relaxed and able to calm her emotions from within herself.
It was the loud thud of the Church doors closing from behind her which startled Mary from her thoughts. Turning round she was expecting to see Father Mulhern, as he normally came to admire her flower arranging and thank her for her services but she could not see anyone.

"Probably hearing things "she muttered to

herself, although she would have sworn it had been the closing of the doors which had broken her thoughts, had she not been in the Lords house.

"Oh no…" he inwardly kicked himself. As Charlie had entered the Church he had not noticed the woman at first and as the large heavy wooden doors had banged shut behind him, he had to be quick on his feet to duck beneath the back pew and lie flat. The last thing he wanted was some old biddy asking interfering questions.

"Oh there you are Father…" stated Mary as Father Mulhern walked casually out from the side room off the Alter.

"I was wondering if I could have a minute of your time Father". She asked as she made her way towards him as he exited the Alter and made for the direction of the pews at the front of the Church. "Of course Mary….anything I can for you….you know that.." the Priest replied smoothly, although inwardly the anxiety he felt every time he was in the vicinity of the woman was pressing upwards so much so that he felt he was going to choke on it.

Mary entered the side of the pew and sat next to him.

"What can I do for you my Dear?" he asked as he moved, turning to look her straight in the face.

"Father…I've been thinking about Gerrard and everything that happened to him, not only the accident but before it, you see, I had this feeling Father that there was something bothering him and I wish I had asked him outright because then I might have been able to help him Father."

Mary paused for breath, as she could feel herself trying to get everything out of her head too quickly, she was aware that the Priest would put her thoughts and ideas down as an over anxious Mother and not take her seriously.

Mary needed for him to take her very seriously because she was certain that there had been something going on within Gerrard and she was certain she would find out with or without this man's help.

Sitting next to Mary he could feel his heart

beating fast he was almost certain she could hear it!

"I'm sure if there had been anything, anything at all Mary… Gerrard would have spoken to you or your husband, I mean you were such a close family unit ", he tried appeasing her in the hope it would reassure her and stop the conversation because he sure didn't like where this could go.
 He could see the tears forming in the corners of Mary's eyes and he began to relax slightly,
"But that's just it Father… I can't help feel I'm being punished for things in the past……, if I hadn't put my baby boy up for adoption all those years ago and broken my family unit then, then maybe all this terrible stuff wouldn't have happened to me and my family now" tears streamed from Mary's eyes as she sat shaking with all the pent up emotions she had been trying so hard to keep intact deep inside her.
 Father Mulhern gently took hold of Mary's hand,
" Mary what happened in the past is the past, it has no control over what happens to you now or in the future, its finished

with and you did what you believed at the time to be the best thing for everyone concerned, especially baby Charlie ",he had to try and calm Mary as best he could, although he could see the pain and agony she was in , he had to nip this in the bud because she was losing it and he couldn't afford for any more casualties.

Minutes passed and Mary slowly began gathering herself together, she had not meant for the conversation to go in this direction but she had been thinking more and more recently about her past and the repercussions which it could be having on her life today.
Mary wiped her eyes and reminded herself of the real reasons she was sat here next to the Father and the questions she wanted his answers to.

" Father do you think Gerrard could have been getting bullied or anyone trying to hurt him in any other way ? " there she had asked it...the one question she desperately wanted the answer to and one which she strongly believed he had the answer to.

Mary looked the Priest straight in the eye as she finished the question and she did not miss the color drain from his face or the slight movement away from her.

The reaction to this question from the man sat next to her made Mary even more certain that he knew something he wasn't telling her about her Son Gerrard and his accident and she was adamant that she would find out exactly what it was he was hiding.

He knew by the look on her face that time was running out for him and his secrets.

" Mary, why on earth would anyone have bullied Gerrard, sure he was the nicest boy and had plenty friends, I'm sure you're just being paranoid now Dear " he was aware he sounded patronizing, but if that's what it was going to take to shut this woman up, then that's what he would do.

The rage was soaring within Mary and she wanted to hit out at him, but she was clever enough to realize that in order for her to take this further she would need to appease him at the moment let him think he was right and get out of there as fast as her legs would take her.

" I'm sure your right Father, I think everything is just getting on top of me and I'm not thinking clearly, I'll just clear away then I'll be off home, thanks for listening " she said as she stood and walked towards the rubbish from her flower arranging and quickly gathering it all up she almost ran from the Church.

As he lay at the back of the Church almost beneath the last pew Charlie could hardly believe what he has just heard.

 He could feel his heart racing like a drum beat and was sure he was hyperventilating as he tried to calm his breathing down. Minutes passed before he had regulated his breathing and was able to get up from where he had been lying. Standing now he felt the blood pump around
his body again as he looked for the woman who had been talking to the Priest who now sat himself at the front of the Alter alone. Slowly and trying not to make noise from his footfall, he made his way towards the

man, who by all means he was sure held the answers to many secrets, especially his own.

Father Mulhern sat praying asking the Lord for forgiveness and to help lead him forward from the situation he had gotten himself into when he heard footsteps which stopped at the end of the pew he sat in.

 At first he thought Mary had returned with more awkward questions but when he looked up and saw who was making their way to sit next to him, he would have warmly welcomed Mary and her questions any day of the week.

"Well! Well! Well! Father "Charlie stated as he made his way to sit next to the man, the Priest's pallor was grey and he was sweating profusely and looked as though he had just saw a ghost.
 Charlie punched him on the shoulder as though they were two old friends meeting for the first time in a while before sitting himself at the side of him and looking into the face his Mother looked into moments before.

"You got something you'd like to confess Father? "He goaded the Priest, well aware he had the upper hand.

Father Mulhern used his tongue to wipe the sweat which had formed on his top lip and looked away from Charlie. He did not want to be sat here with this person for a variety of reasons but mainly because he knew what Charlie was capable of if he lost his temper, as he had used this to his benefit previously.

" The way I see it FATHER....you have been a naughty boy in more ways than one and now's your chance to ask forgiveness, I mean you're in the right place, RIGHT ! ", shouted Charlie moving his face closer to the Priests so that he could smell the rancid breathe of the man.

" You have nothing on me, you reprobate ! " , spat the Priest back in Charlie's face, as he moved sideways trying to gauge how far he would have to run to get away from him.

He had quickly worked it out in his mind that Charlie might think he had him, but all he knew was that he had the answers to Charlie's Mothers whereabouts, hence the reason he had been so keen to help the Priest with a little problem he had.

Charlie saw the quick glance the Priest had made to the side of the pew and laughed out loud.

"You seriously think you are going to get away from me old man. . .Not a chance...You my man have some talking to do, so START TALKING ! ", he screamed as he grabbed the Priest by the scruff of his neck and shoved him out of the pew towards the back of the Church.

Once Charlie had got him to the back of the Church he pushed him into the small room which was used by the caretaker where he was certain they would not be disturbed.

Charlie threw Father Mulhern onto the floor and looking around found some gaffer tape which had been the nearest thing to his hand,
    "See, even the good Lord thinks it's about

time you lightened your soul, making things sooo accessible " , he laughed as he used the tape to tie the Priests hands and feet together,

"There …you aren't going anywhere, anytime soon, now are you "Charlie joked at the Priest as he finished with the tape and threw it over his shoulder.

Father Mulhern was trying to remain as relaxed as he possibly could so that the pain from the tightness of the tape on his wrists would go away, however, this was not working and the pain from his wrists swelling was becoming unbearable. He realized this was only go one way and that it would not be his.

CHAPTER FIFTEEN

As Vicki and Carol were coming out of the newsagents they spotted Mrs. Donachy.

"Hey Carol, look ...over there, there's Gerrard's Mum "stated Vicki as she unwrapped the chocolate bar she had just bought.
 Carol nodded and looked in the direction

of Mrs. Donachy, before quickly looking back at Vicki, who now had chocolate all around her mouth. Shaking her head and laughing at her friend's predicament Carol wondered how at 14 Vicki still managed to get into such a state eating chocolate.

Pointing at her mouth and making a wiping movement Carol instructed Vicki to clean her mouth before they walked across the road just in front of Mrs. Donachy. Both girls could see the redness around Mrs. Donachy's eyes and looked at one another with a slight shrug of their shoulders, as they approached the woman.

" Hello Mrs. Donachy " said Carol, as they stopped in front of the woman it was more apparent that she had been crying a lot recently, as her eyes were all red and her skin blotchy.
Mrs. Donachy looked like a bag of nerves standing in front of them and they both felt heart sorry for her at the troubles she had faced in the past few months.

"Are you alright there Mrs. Donachy "? Enquired Vicki as she stood looking into the woman's face before her.

"Uch... I'll be fine girl, think I'm having a bad day, that's all "

Mary was taken aback at the girl's show of concern and was eager to get away, as she felt stupid enough without the young girls seeing her like this as well.

"It's no wonder after everything you've been through Mrs. Donachy, it's only natural, as me Mum would say "replied Carol, trying to comfort the woman as much as she knew how to.

Vicki pulled Carol's sleeve and was nodding towards Mrs. Donachy, who with her head bowed was oblivious to the goings on, as Vicki eagerly encouraged Carol to keep talking. Carol did not need to be told what it was Vicki was hinting at and pushing her to ask, Carol was still unsure about them looking into Jonjo and Gerrard's deaths and thought it best left to the professionals, but Vicki and John were adamant that they were the ones to solve the mysteries.

"Mrs. Donachy please don't think I'm being nosey, cos I aint, but we were just wondering if you knew of any reason why

this would have happened to Gerrard? Asked Vicki outright.
 Carol could have slapped her friend there and then had it not been for the woman's speedy reply,
"What do you mean...Do you know what it was? "

Both Carol and Vicki looked from Mrs. Donachy to each other with puzzled expressions on their faces.
" What do you know girls, you have to tell me, so that I can find out what exactly happened to my boy, please " Carol and Vicki could hear the pleading in Mrs. Donachy's voice and as they looked at each other they knew they had to tell Gerrard's Mum everything they knew and help her in getting to the truth.

Mary Donachy could not believe that she was not the only one with doubts regards the truth about the death of her beautiful son.
 The fact that these two young girls stood in front of her asking the same question which had been going around and around inside her own head was nothing short of a

miracle she felt.

"Where are you girls off to at the moment "she asked as she did not want to let them go without talking some more.
" We weren't going any place in particular ", Vicki replied, knowing that her Mum would think she was at Carols and vice versa, as this always worked for them both as their cover story should they need one.

"Do you fancy a juice? We could go the café in town if you like to talk ". Mary tried to keep the desperation from her voice so that she would not frighten the girls off, unaware that they were as eager to speak to her as she was to them.

After they had been served with their drinks Vicki Carol and Mrs. Donachy sat around a small round table in the back of the café hoping that no-one would see and disturb them.

"So.... let me get this straight ", began Mary, who could not quite believe what the girls had finished telling her, "This boy has told you that Jonjo was being sexually abused by Father Mulhern and he wasn't the only one, So you think he was murdered because of this"?
The fact that the girls had confirmed her worst fears sent shivers throughout her body.

Vicki and Carol sat nodding in agreement, but Mary could see the disbelief in their faces that she was taking them and their investigations seriously.

"We have asked Vicki's Brother John to try and find out if any of the other boys will talk, we told him to pretend he wants to become an Alter boy.... ", explained Carol, "I know they might not say but it's only going to take one to say and we can go the Police"
Vicki realized that the boys were not just going to come out and tell John but they

lived in hope, if not they didn't know how else they would get evidence against the Priest.

" Listen girls, I have been thinking about my Gerrard and the way he was acting before what happened to him and I know there was certainly something wrong with him, call it Mother's intuition "
Mary knew this could be the beginning of the end for Father Mulhern if they could find the evidence required to prove these allegations.
Both girls sat in silence as the enormity of the situation dawned on them and they silently wished they had left this in the hands of the professionals because they did not have a good feeling about how this would end.

The three of them sat in silence around the small table as they individually played out in their own minds how where and what was going to happen from this point.

It was Vicki who broke the silence, "I think the best thing is to contact the Police now and tell them everything we know" she stated, looking more worried than she had half an hour before.

"Vicki I think we should inform the Police but I think we need more information before they'll believe us "replied Mary who realized she needed to confront Father Mulhern before anyone else got the chance as she had more to hide than them.

As the girls had divulged their information they had collected, Mary felt sick at the thought of anyone forcing her Son in any way never mind sexually.

This had soon turned to rage and the desire to harm the Priest was growing with every second she spent sitting in the café. The desire to harm the Priest was quenched when she thought of the way in which he had helped her and her secret which he could and would probably divulge should she confront him regards these allegations, but she told herself she could not afford to let this information go unnoticed or him unharmed !

Once the girls had left Mary Donachy they felt a bit better in the knowledge that they now had an adult as an ally and this reassured them that they had done the right thing and it would soon be over.

On reaching Vicki's house they ran in the front door with her shouting out,
 "It's us Mum, that's us in for the night "as Carol was staying the night, since it was the weekend and they often slept over at each other's house. John was lying in the living room watching tv when he heard Vicki's holler, getting to his feet he ran down the hallway to his sister's bedroom.

 Upon entering he heard them mention Mrs. Donachy and realized they had divulged their theory to her.
 "No way have you spoke to her ", he cried in disbelief, as he jumped onto the bed bedside the girls.
Vicki shoved him so that he fell into Carol,
 "Well we have AND she believed us...in fact she was already thinking the Priest was involved with something shady anyway "she cried almost in a childlike way. John

shook his head and asked, "So what's she going to do about it then smarty?"

Carol could see this was going to end up in the two siblings arguing so she replied, " she is going to think this through then inform the Police...I think " she sounded more sure than she felt because she thought she sensed that Mary Donachy had other things to discuss with the Priest.

"Well at least an adult knows and we can't be blamed for not doing anything about what we know "John agreed with his sister, they would just wait and see what happened next and hope it all turned out okay.

At least now he might not be the person blamed for Gerrard running into the path of that lorry and dying, if they were right then the Priest could have more to answer for this than himself, he closed his eyes and prayed.

CHAPTER SIXTEEN

In the caretakers room within the Church
the Priest was sending up his own prayers,
promising the Lord that if he helped him to

get out of this room alive he would stop abusing the boys and spend the rest of his life doing nothing but good.

When he caught sight of Charlie with a Stanley knife and a dangerous glint in his eyes, he knew his prayers had not been answered and the Lord and turned his back on him.

"Right... you pathetic coward... "spat out Charlie moving closer towards Father Mulhern,

"You are going to tell me what I want to know then I'll decide where we go from there...COMPRENDE!" he waved the Stanley knife in front of the Priests face. "I'm going to give you one chance, and one chance only to confess to me your sins, then I'll think about how you're going to pay for them...UNDERSTAND FATHER " ?

Father Mulhern was shaking with fear and the sweat was blinding him as he lay on the floor tied up.
He knew he had met his match in Charlie the moment that he set eyes upon him all those months ago and he now wished he had denied all knowledge of the

information which he was after, at this moment he felt he had bargained with the Devil and this one the Devil was going to win.

Charlie could see he had the man terrified and thought so he should be......

After all he had heard and saw within this community for which the Priest was supposed to guide, he knew there was underhanded guiding going on from the Priest as he took advantage of his position within the community, he would make it his business to find out why the Priest had been so keen for him to take care of the fella he now knew was Jonjo McNeil but first he had his own questions he needed the answers to.

Sitting on the floor in front of the Priest, Charlie stared the man straight in the face,

" You told me you knew where my biological Mother was and you were going to provide me with her name, that was the agreement, but from hearing your little discussion with THAT woman I would say I'VE found out where my Mother is......Wouldn't you agree ? "

" I don't know what you're talking about "
Father Mulhern was not going to make this
easy for this thug and he already thought
he was not going to come out of this in one
piece or even alive.

"I'm sure I heard her plead with you about
her baby she had given away and unless
you advice all your precious parishioners to
give up their babies, I would say that there
is a good chance her baby was me! "

"What you saying old man? Cat got your
tongue now? Or have you realized in that
sick head of yours that I've worked this
thing out for myself...."

Charlie had known the minute he had
heard the woman talk of her baby which
she had given away that this could be the
woman he had spent most of his adult life
searching for. When she had stated that
the baby's name was Charlie he could not
stop his heart and mind from racing at the
possibility that this was IT, the moment he
dreamt about since he had been told from
his adoptive parents, he could not wait to
meet this woman nor for her to give the
answers he had done anything to hear,

including murder!

As Father Mulhern lay helplessly on the floor listening to Charlie he had no reason to withhold the information about Mary any longer.

The fact that Charlie had been hiding in the Church and had heard what he and Mary had been discussing, he could do nothing but nod his head at the words coming from Charlie. He felt defeated and the fight had left him because he was under no illusion how this was going to end, at least he told himself, he would have done some good in reuniting Mary with her Son before meeting his maker.
 He startled as Charlie got to his feet and began pacing up and down in the tiny space in front of getting more and more agitated with every passing second.

"Yes, yes...You are right in what you say.....That woman is your Mother "!

He did not miss the look of relief which had come over Charlie's face and felt a little bit of hope that he may survive this ordeal somehow, as Charlie stopped pacing and slumped down onto the floor in front of the Priest once more.

The young man's demeanor softened ever so slightly at what the Priest was praying was going to be a change of heart in his plans towards himself, however, this was short lived as Charlie looked at him with menace in his eyes again.

"What is her name? Where does she live "? He realized that once he had provided these answers then the young man had no use for him and this ordeal would soon be over...
"Her name is Mary Donachy and she lives here in Hollowburn ....432 Cart Road"

Inside Charlie felt overwhelmed with the fact he now had his answers and could not wait to go in search of the woman who had given him life.

Although he felt relief and joy at eventually gaining this information Charlie still had unfinished business with the man in front of him........

"This isn't over yet old man...You still have

your own confession to make "
"I've told you her name and where you can find her. What more do you want? It all happened a long time ago and she had nowhere to turn to....."

He was well aware this was not what Charlie was looking for but he'd be damned if he was going to tell him what he had been doing with the boys who served the parish as Alter boys.
 There were some secrets that must be taken to the grave with you, and this, he felt, was one of them.

At that moment they both heard the slam of the church doors and Father Martin prayed that it was someone who could help him out of this scenario before he was tortured to death because as he had found out from previous experience with Charlie, he did not stop until the red mist cleared.

"Damn "thought Charlie, just as things

were getting interesting. He would need to make sure the Priest kept quiet now the last thing he needed was some busybody getting caught up in his plans.

Pointing to the Priest to keep quiet he slowly and as quietly as he could crept over to retrieve the gaffer tape he had thrown, after he had used it on the old man's hands and feet, now he placed a large piece over the Priests mouth ensuring that he could not attract any unwanted attention towards the room.

CHAPTER SEVENTEEN

Mary was like a woman on a mission now that she had information to back up her gut instincts she was determined to let the

Priest know what she had found out and ensure he paid for what he had done, especially to her beloved Son.

Walking up towards the church she was full of anger and frustration keen to get answers as to why a man of God and in his position could act in the manner which he had, taking advantage of his position within the community and with the young boys....
No way was she going to let this go, she fully intended confronting the Priest straight out!

Entering the church Mary usually took care not to bang the church doors as to bring attention to herself also so as not to disturb anyone who was already in praying.

However, today she was too angry and hurt to think of anyone other than the man she had come to see and it was not the one on the cross today.
 Although she did think to herself, she wouldn't mind putting the bloody Priest on a cross herself!
 Mary chastised herself for having such thoughts and especially in the church, but

then again she thought, WHY NOT!!!

The church was quiet and there was no-one seated or kneeling in the pews, this was good she thought to herself, as she didn't want any distractions for herself or the Father.

 No...Today she wanted him all to herself!

Walking towards the Alter all she could hear were the squeaks coming from her shoes on the parquet floor, and she inhaled the smell of incense as she tried to calm her breathing in preparation for confronting the Priest.

 Usually, the smell of the incense and the stillness of the church with the warm colors from the stain glassed windows shining through filled her with a sense of peace, but not today.

Mary feared that she would never find peace within the church again now that she knew what had happened here and what the Priest had done.

Part of her frustration was believing in the church and holding it in a place of such high regard, not to mention all the time and energy she had spent doing what she thought was the best for the place and the man.

Oh what a fool she had been.....Then she thought...Not just myself and family but all the other people affected by this betrayal, she feared for the future of the church within the community once this became common knowledge, and she would ensure it did become exactly that.

Mary searched all over the inside of the church looking in the rooms off the Alter and to the side she could not find the Priest anywhere. She had already called the housekeeper to find out if the Priest was in his house today but the housekeeper had informed her that he was not out on business today and could be found in the church, therefore, Mary couldn't understand where he had gotten to.

Exiting the inner church she checked the toilet door, it was open and she checked inside, no sighn of anyone.....

Strange she thought....

Knowing that the caretaker was still on holiday she thought maybe the Priest had gone into his room looking for something.

Approaching the door Mary thought that she heard muffles coming from inside,

"Hello, anyone in there, Father Mulhern...Are you in here? "She enquired as she tried turning the door handle, to no avail, the handle was stuck and she couldn't shift it.

This doesn't feel right she told herself, she was beginning to feel dread that maybe she had disturbed the Priest during an illicit act with one of the young boys or worse.

Panic and then anger set in as she told

herself she would just have to be strong and find out what exactly was going on the other side of the door.

"Hello Father can you answer me please, Are you alright ? " she felt sick at the thought of even asking the man this question unsure of what was going on the other side of the door, but she did not know any other way to play this out until she got the door unlocked.

Still no answer, she was certain that there was someone in that room,

"Father if you don't answer me I shall have to go phone for help" just as the last word had left her lips the door opened and an arm grabbed her neck catapulting her towards the other side of the door.

Seeing the Priest lying on the floor all tied up was the first thing Mary lay her eyes on. The Priest's eyes were bulging and his face was scarlet as he was not able to breathe properly due to the gaffer tape across his mouth.

Mary fell to the floor beside him and removed the tape still unaware of who was standing behind her, her first instinct had been to help the Priest who was struggling for air and she could not have his death on her conscience.

The tape came off with ease and the Priest was gasping for air as she turned to try and pull him up into a seated positon, it was then Mary noticed the young man with the knife standing in front of them now.

Mary looked at the young man then looked again........

At first she thought she was seeing things probably due the stress of the circumstances, but... NO... there was no mistaken THOSE eyes and THAT mouth, not to mention the nose, the cheekbones, she looked straight into the face of Charlie Delaney.

Mary could not believe what she was seeing!

Charlie stood staring at the woman he had seen earlier with the Priest talking about her baby she had given away and a hundred and one different emotions went through him.

The one emotion which was at the forefront of them all was confusion.

Confusion that the woman in front of him, who looked so nice and warmly, could have given up her baby.

Confusion that the woman in front of him had basically fell into this situation and was seeing him for the first time with a knife pointed at her, this was not the first impression he wanted her to have of him. He had to think fast to try and fix this because he had waited far too long for this meeting to be anything other than perfect, and at this precise moment it was far from that.

"Mary.... Mary, thank god you're here..... ",
gasped the Priest still lying on the floor,
"He is going to kill me....Help me!!! ", the
Priest was hysterical now as Mary and
Charlie watched him as his tears were
meeting the snot which fell from is nose, he
was a weeping mess.

It was more disbelief at the situation she
had found herself in than anything else
which prevented Mary from screaming and
hitting out at the man that she had come
to despise.
 Looking at the groveling wreck in front of
her she felt pity but she would not let this
overcome the feelings of rage she had when
she thought of what he had done to her
other Son.

Taking a deep breathe Mary got her feet
and stood in front of who she believed to be
HER Charlie extending her hand she
quietly said,
"If, I'm right by looking in your eyes, I
believe I am your Mother, the woman who
birthed you.....Is your name still Charlie?"

The tears fell from her eyes as she struggled to steady her hand and her voice as they were shaking so much, the young man put the knife on the shelf behind him and took her hand.

"Yes.... my name is still Charlie and I have been looking for you for a long time now, I'm sorry we had to meet like this but this so called Priest has a lot to answer for and I hope you can grant me the forgiveness for what he has made me do..." pleaded Charlie, hoping that his Mother would not hold this against him and turn her back on him again.

Instinctively, Mary threw her arms around Charlie and drew him into her. It felt so good and so right hugging him close and smelling him she was sure there was nothing that she could not forgive him.

Moments passed with them embracing each other when the spell was broken by the sound of the Priests' whimpering. Charlie stepped back slightly from Mary's embrace and felt reassured that this woman would not let him down again, he hoped for all their sakes that he was right, because they still had the Priest to deal with first.

Mary gave a silent nod of her head and Charlie took this as her understanding that there were issues which needed dealing with first before they could have the reunion which they both desired.

CHAPTER EIGHTEEN

Lying looking up at Mother and Son embracing each other he realized he had lost all his bargaining chips in one swift go. Now that Mary had found Charlie, all be it not in the best possible way, he was left with no more cards to deal them, he just prayed and hoped they would not be so hard on him.

He was shocked when it was Mary who attacked him first, he was certain now that she had her precious son she would disappear and hopefully take the thug with her, but this seemed something of a pipe dream by the way in which she was lashing out at him.

" You...you piece of scum !!" she was screaming as the rage returned to her, now that she had Charlie back in her life it had magnified the loss of her Gerrard and she was not going to let this scumbag get away with it !

"You had me give away one of my Sons and you took away my other Son...I know what you've been up to with the young boys and I know it was because of you my Gerrard died " she was screaming at the top of her lungs whilst thrashing at him with all the might she could muster.

"How could you " ? , she repeatedly asked as she hit the Priest over and over, " YOU ! ,are a man of the cloth, YOU ! ,are supposed to help people and help me, but, YOU are a liar and a dirty old man " Mary bashed her fists repeatedly against the man's head and body, as she allowed her rage to unfold from inside her,

"We trusted you…you're nothing but a pervert and you…YOU….killed my boy "!

The Priest was trying hard to cover his face from the throws Mary was providing but because of the way his hands and feet were taped together he was a sitting duck, he could not protect himself from this woman's rage.

Charlie stood totally a taken back by the way in which his Mother was lashing out at the old man on the floor, but he was not prepared for the words which had left her mouth, these accusations hit a nerve with him, because now he understood what it was the Priest was trying to cover up by having him do what he had done to Jonjo McNeil.

He had abused the boy and was scared he would be found out if the boy spoke, so had blackmailed him into silencing him.

Charlie felt sick to his stomach at what the old man had been doing but more so at what he had done to the poor boy.
The fact that his Mother was accusing the Priest of abusing the boy was bad enough only now Charlie realized the implications towards the other boys and one of them being his Brother, HIS Brother whom he would not meet or get to know, because he had taken that away from him. This infuriated Charlie and he felt the red mist descend upon him once more.

"Vicki do you not think we should go see

Mrs. Donachy and find out if she has said anything to the Priest yet "?

Carol was sitting on the stairs in the hallway at her house using the telephone, she had to be quick before her Mum latched onto this fact and shouted at her to get off.

What was the point on having a phone if you couldn't use it, was that not the whole point she always asked when ordered off, but this was an argument she would never win so she preferred to be sneaky about calling her friend.

Carol felt they should have heard from Mrs. Donachy before now and was keen to find out if she had more information for them to pass onto the Police.

"Yeah, probably, you would think she's had long enough, hasn't she? I'll meet you at the chippy in ten minutes, my treat " Carol quickly returned the phone to the table it sat on, grabbed her coat and ran out the front door yelling " I'm away out, not be long," she could almost taste the chips she was going to get.

Vicki was standing at the chip shops door
waiting on her when she approached her
the smell of freshly fried chips and vinegar
wafted so strongly they both almost ran to
the counter to make their order.
Both girls looked forward to a chippy treat
as they both loved chips and the fact you
ate them on the go whilst they kept your
hands warm was an added bonus never
lost on the girls as they walked around
looking for talent usually to chat up,
tonight though was a different case all
together.

Reaching the Donachys' house they started
arguing over who should start the talking,
Vicki lost and wasted no time in knocking
the big white door.

  Mr. Donachy answered the door after a few
knocks on the door and his quizzical look
wasn't lost on either girl.

"Hi, Mr. Donachy, sorry to bother you, but
can we speak to Mrs. Donachy please?"
asked Vicki in her politest voice she had. At
her side she could feel Carol sniggering as

her shoulders shrugged up and down at her acting.

This did not help ease her feeling of apprehension when Mr. Donachy explained that his wife was not at home and had last gone to the church on business a couple of hours earlier. Vicki thanked Mr. Donachy and quickly made their excuses to leave.

As they walked down the path the each girl could feel the panic rise in their chest, turning looking into one another face they acknowledged without words their need for speed in getting to the church as fast as possible, they began running.

The church was illuminated from the outside as it was early evening and looked beautiful and serene but they both sensed that it might not be serene inside, as they opened the church door the sound of falling steel and shouting almost made the girls turn around and run, if only they could.

The sound of screaming was becoming louder as they approached the door on their right hand side, whispering, Carol

leaned near Vicki's ear,
"Vicks I think we need to get the Police and
NOW "!

Vicki looked her straight in the face and
she sensed that there was no way her
friend was going anywhere, if there was one
thing Vicki liked it was drama and she
would never turn and run from this,
however much she hoped she would.

" No chance, did you not hear those
screams, someone's in trouble, Carol we
can't just turn and run, we might be able
to help " Vicki's face was flushed with
excitement and Carol accepted her chance
of running was over, she was stuck here
with her friend, she would not leave Vicki
on her own.

"Right you push open the door after three "
Vicki instructed her, " I'll go in once you
open the door and you better come straight
in after me , Promise ? "
"Yeah, promise "she agreed, as the linked
their little pinky fingers in securing their
promise to each other, this was what they
called the pinky promise and NO-ONE
broke a pinky promise.

Vicki counted to three and Carol pushed open the heavy walnut door allowing her partner to push into the room at her back. The scene which met their eyes was one nightmares were made of......

"OH MY GOD! OH MY GOD! OH MY GOD! "The girls repeatedly screamed, waving their arms about having totally lost all their calm composure, as they saw the body of Father Mulhern lying all twisted in a pool of his blood on the floor.

At the side kneeling over him was Mrs. Donachy , with her face and hands covered in blood, shaking and screaming, when she became aware of the girls in the room she looked up at them both and screamed louder.

All around them both were stainless steel bowls which were used for the offertory and other bits and pieces from the sacramental process which took place at every mass.

The room was boiling warm and the smell of sweat and blood was thick and heavy, Carol felt that she was going throw up and was swallowing hard to prevent her from vomiting on top of the Priests body there in front of her at her feet.

The sight of Mrs Donachy kneeling at the side of the Priest covered in blood Vicki assumed that the woman had confronted the man and had lost the plot, resulting in this scene of carnage in front of her.

"Mrs. Donachy........." The woman stopped screaming and looked up, Vicki thought she was staring at her but then suddenly she became aware of a figure standing behind her and she felt as if her legs were going to give way leaving her on the floor next to the bloody body.

Carol gasped and pointed behind Vicki....

Upon turning Vicki came face to face with the person she saw on the night Jonjo had been murdered, the figure which had been hiding under the archway, was now in full view standing in front of her, with a knife in his hand, which was dripping with blood.

"YOU....OH MY GOD ", exclaimed Vicki, totally stunned.

This was not making any sense to her at all, Gerrard Donachy was dead but the person stood here has such a resemblance to him, she could not get her head around this and was beginning to feel totally out of her depths.

Seeing her friend's reaction to the man standing in the small room Carol knew Vicki had not imagined seeing Gerard under the archway on the night of Jonjo's murder.

Whoever this person was he was Gerrard's double and even as he stood staring at them she was having difficulty piecing all this together, her brain could not comprehend what she was seeing and what she knew as fact.

Carol's head was beginning to feel dizzy, she felt her legs go weak and collapsed onto the cold floor beneath, just opposite the lifeless body of Father Mulhern.

CHAPTER NINETEEN

As Mary Donachy looked up and around the small room she could not believe the carnage before her eyes.

Lying in front of her was the lifeless body of the man she had trusted and depended upon for most of her life, and discovering the lengths which he had gone to in order to safe himself from destruction within the community, she realized she never knew him...NOT the REAL him !

The first thing which brought Mary back to the room was the horrific screams coming from Vicki as she watches her friend Carol slump to the ground in front of them.

" Vicki.....Vicki....calm down I think she has just fainted.... ", says Mary as calmly as she could, she didn't wish to raise her voice or scream herself as she so wanted to.

Mary slowly got to her feet and crossed the small room to get to Carol, she checked her neck for a pulse and confirmed that Carol had indeed fainted.

As she looked up to reassure Vicki, who is frozen in fear, Mary notices the blood covered hands in front of her and it hits her then that they are HER hands and she passes out on the floor next to Carol.

Staring, unable to move, Vicki is telling herself to get a grip, "this must be a nightmare, I'll wake up shortly ", she repeats over and over in her head, until her lips begin to move and she realizes she is not sleeping and can hear her words aloud from inside her head.

"You're right, this is a nightmare, but, let me assure you, you are not dreaming girl "comes a deep, chilling voice from behind her.

Vicki's heart is racing and she can feel the sweat dripping from her body as she slowly turns to face the Gerrard lookalike standing there.
One good thing, she thinks to herself, he has put the knife down, however, her eyes are automatically drawn to the blood stained clothes and hands in front of her.

Ironic as it seems to Vicki she is praying nonstop in her head that help will arrive soon and she's still alive to see it.
Vicki realizes that it was her which had gotten herself and her best friend in this situation, so she must try and get them out of it ALIVE.

"Are you going to hurt me "? Vicki sheepishly asks Charlie, all he can see are her eyes from beneath her eyelashes, as she dare not look directly into his face.

Charlie at first doesn't quite know how to answer this as he is still trying to figure out a way to escape from this room, however, he also realizes that to run away he would lose the one person he had spent his life craving and searching for....HIS MOTHER!

Assessing the scene before him he decides he must try and salvage something from this mess.....

"No, I'm not going to hurt you, but you must help me try and awaken these two here "Charlie states, nodding towards Carol and Mary Donachy.

The relief in Vicki's face is clear for him see and he knows that the people within this room are not the danger, it is once they leave this room that the real trouble will begin.

Vicki moves quickly over towards Carol and

Mary Donachy, speaking gently asking
them to wake up and gently shakes them
and rubs their arms, until eventually they
both come to, albeit, still extremely shaken.

" Carol ", whispers Vicki into her friends
ear, " Carol, You need to stay calm and try
help us get out of here alive, he says he
won't hurt us " Vicki tries to reassure
Carol, although she can still see the fear in
her face.
Carol slowly nods her head and begins to
get to her feet.

 Once she has Carol on her feet again they
both assist Mary Donachy up onto hers
although she still seems unsteady on her
feet, so the girls encourage her to sit
upright against the wall, allowing them
time to try figure out a plan.

"I think he is telling the truth Carol, I don't
think he will hurt us "whispers Vicki, "I
know it's a big risk but we don't have any
choice really, do we "? Vicki leaves the
question hanging as she walks over to
check on Mary Donachy.

 Carol now feeling slightly calmer than

before averts her eyes upwards as she knows the Priests bloody body is close to her feet, given the size of the room, there is nothing else she can do which will help give her the focus to get out of here, and she definitely needs all the focus she can summons at the moment.

"You do understand that I did not want any of this don't you "? Charlie is kneeling beside his Mother.
 Mary is sitting upright against the wall staring straight ahead, Charlie isn't even sure if she can hear him as he suspects she has gone into shock, but this doesn't stop him trying to explain.
Suddenly, Mary turns and looks directly into his eyes, nods her head and returns to staring straight ahead once more.
Charlie decides to leave her be and concentrates on escaping the mess within this room.

Charlie gets to his feet and turns towards the two young girls who are standing staring at him, probably wondering as much as he is, as to how they get out of this in one piece.

"I'm not going to hurt anyone, I didn't even want to hurt him but he made it impossible not to, given everything he has done to my family and I now understand others, as well "Charlie explains to Carol and Vicki, hoping to ease their fears.
  Both girls were as white as ghosts but Charlie realized they had some guts, or they would not be here in the first place, therefore he was relying on this to help them all through this.

"Your family "? Enquired Vicki, "Does that mean that you ARE related to Gerrard Donachy "? Vicki was quickly joining the dots in her mind, regards the similarity in looks between Gerrard and this guy in front of her.

  Looking sideways towards Carol she was hoping that her friend was putting everything together as well, although this placed a massive question mark over the man in front of them, in this room with them AND the night Jonjo was murdered. This understanding was beginning to really freak Vicki as she was certain that she and

Carol were standing in front of Jonjo's murderer!

"It's a long story but yes I am related and did not want any of this to happen to anyone, I only wanted to find my Mother and.............."

Charlie never got to finish his sentence as the room door were flung open and the small room became overrun with Police brandishing guns.
 There was a lot of shouting
 "GET DOWN...... GET DOWN....."From the Police, "HANDS BEHIND YOU HEAD "!

Instruction left right and centre, Vicki and Carol became hysterical and followed the instructions, they would do anything to get out and home to the safety of their families.

CHAPTER TWENTY

2 MONTHS LATER

As Carol lay in her bed listening to the rain and wind batter outside her bedroom window she tossed and turned, but she just could not get back to sleep no matter what she tried.

Ever since THAT day Carol had not been able to sleep properly, whenever she would try to get some sleep, when she closed her eyes all she could see was the blood covered lifeless body of the Priest, and she would quickly open her sleepy eyes and just lie there, wishing for the daylight to come through her curtains. During the day Carol remained in the safety of her house and had taken sanctuary there since she had returned home once the Police and Hospital had released them.

Lying thinking about what had happened she was glad that they had uncovered the truth about Jonjo's murder and Gerrard's accident. Carol and Vicki were both being hailed as heroes within the local community, but a hero was the last thing Carol felt she was.

There was a knock at her bedroom door......

"Carol, is it ok if I come in "? It was her big Sister Tracy.

Carol knew that her Sister and Mum were worried sick about her and had made a promise with herself and them to try come out her room more and involve herself in the family again.

"Yeah, sure come in "she replied, as Tracy tip toed across the room. Carol felt her Sister sit on the edge of her bed so turned towards her.

" Listen wee one, me and Mum are really worried about you, will you please get ready and come sit with us in the living room " ? Pleaded Tracy, as she took Carol's hand into hers.

" Every time I close my eyes I see HIM ! "
sobbed Carol as her Sister stroked her arm,
Tracy stopped what she was doing and
bent to cradle her Sister in a warm
embrace, whispering reassurances into her
ear, hoping to ease her wee Sisters
anguish.
Both Sisters sat embraced in the safe
knowledge that they would get through this
together, with the help of their Mum and
one another.

Minutes passed then they heard the phone
ringing.......

"Carol....." called her Mum from the
hallway, "Vicki's on the phone for you..."

Carol looked up into her Sister's face and
thought this was as good a time as any to
get out of her bed and join the real world
again, although she realized it was going to
take time to recover from recent events, she
felt more confident that she would.
 After all, she had her Mum, Sister and
Best Friend to help see her through and
the best bit was also that her Dad had been
jailed for a long time after the beating he
had given her Mum, so things were looking

on the bright side already.

Quickly she jumped up and out her bed and ran out to the hallway to speak to her Best Friend.

"About time.....thought you had immigrated to a land faraway Pal "joked Vicki down the phone line.

Although she was joking with Carol, she was worried about her friend and had missed her, as she had not been around lately.

Vicki understood where her friend was and why, she herself, was having problems with sleeping but the Doctors at the Hospital had explained that this might happen and had offered them both counselling services as well.

Therefore, Vicki wasn't worrying too much about her lack of sleep and hoped that as the days passed she would relax more and natural sleep would come again. Everyone was being super supportive and treating the girls like superstars...
Vicki was quite enjoying the attention and

gifts which had been handed into the house for her.

At home, things were getting back to normal, and her Mum although worried about her, was becoming more relaxed and more like herself, as the negative attention which John was receiving from friends and neighbors had withered. Vicki was relieved about this and glad her Mum was happier these days as well as John.

Once she had returned home and had digested all the details of what they discovered in the care takers room, she still could not believe that what had seemed like a far- fetched theory regards the Priest was actually nearer the truth than they ever could have imagined, she was dumb struck!

Never in a million years would she have imagined her and Carol getting embroiled in a 'Nancy Drew 'type thriller. Vicki laughed to herself as she thought of the comment Carol had made way back at the start of the mystery about her thinking she was 'Nancy Drew ' if only she chuckled.

"Do you fancy coming out for some chips, maybe come to mine if you want "? Vicki asked Carol, silently praying that her friend would say yes.

She had really missed her and she also really fancied a bag of chips. Someone had bought her the brand new album from Wham and she could not stop listening to it, she knew Carol would love it too, so if being outside was too much too soon for Carol they would come back here and blast the music, it's the least they deserved after their heroism, she laughed to herself.

"Ok then, will you come meet me then "? replied Carol, she had decided today was the day !
"Yeah no problem Pal, Hey Carol.... remember when you said I thought I was Nancy Drew? Well.... we blooming well were...weren't we "? And all Carol could do was laugh heartily along with her Friend, YES, they would both be fine!

"Are you ready Mary "? Philip called in

from the opened front door.

He was getting used to the 2 hour drives and quite enjoyed the scenery along the way as well as spending time with his Mary, because lately as every day passed Mary was slowly but surely returning to her old self.

The few days after the incident and brutal death of THAT man had been what he could only describe as hell on earth!

On THAT day after the two girls had visited looking for Mary he realized she had been gone quite a while and this was unusual as Mary had her routine and liked the dinner organized and eaten for the same time every day, this she called structure, he called it OCD. However, no matter what they called her 'structure 'it was the reason for her being here today.

Philip became increasingly concerned as time was passing and had grabbed his jacket and made his way towards the Church.

It was as he entered the main front doors Philip heard shouting and sobbing, as he looked around the inside foyer of the Church he realized the noises were coming from the direction of the Care Takers room.

Philip had a feeling that there was something untoward going on within the room and quickly ran to the rectory at the side of the church. Eventually, after banging loudly on the door, the housekeeper answered and he yelled at her to dial 999, explaining the noises and the urgency in which he needed assistance.

To Philip it felt like an hour had gone by as he stood outside the Church he could still hear the shouts and cries of what sounded like women and he was frantic with worry as he paced up and down outside the church doors.

All at once the noise of Police sirens were heard from nearby and then they were in full view as four pulled to an abrupt stop at the gates and he lost count of the number of Officers running past him, he couldn't count them exactly as they ran by so fast, in the direction of the church doors.

Shouting and banging of doors then there was silence......

Forty minutes later Philip felt a relief which he had never experienced before in his life as the church door opened and there, being held up by a woman Police Officer was his Mary, trembling and white with shock, Philip ran towards to greet her and then he saw the blood on her clothes and covering her hands.

"What......Are you ok, are you hurt, Love "? He enquired as he lifted her hands out in front of them both. Mary looked at his face and he saw that she could not bring herself to look at her blood soaked hands.

Lowering her hands Philip asked her again, "Mary, Love ......Are you ok "? This time she looked into his eyes and broke down sobbing.

Philip had not known the true extent of the horrors which had enfolded that day straight away, but as the days came and went, Mary slowly divulged the story as she remembered it.

The most important and life changing part being the reason for their drive out today.

At first Mary was unsure of how to tell Philip about the return of Charlie back into her life, especially after losing their boy, his boy, Gerrard.

The manner in which she had come face to face with her first born Son was still not sitting right in her own mind so how could she possibly expect Philip to accept Charlie was back and more so the fact that she wanted to remain in contact with him.

The attention from the community and the media was overpowering and very intrusive to Mary and Philip who were extremely private people.
Charlie was arrested and charged with the murders of Jonjo McNeil and Father

Mulhern, however, he was placed in remand and is still awaiting trial.

Mary was worried what people would think of her about the fact she had placed Charlie up for adoption, but her worries were unfounded as in today's society being an unmarried Mother was more accepted and now that her story had been told nationwide, there seemed to be a feeling of empathy towards her and what she had endured at the hands of Father Mulhern and the Church.

It angered Mary and Philip that the Priest had played such big parts in her losing her Sons at one time or another.

Thinking back all those years ago when she discovered she was expecting Charlie and placing her faith in the Priest and church she could never have imagined the pain and anguish it would embroil throughout her life, even until now.

The fact that the Priest had been

systematically abusing young boys and her Gerrard being damaged and then killed by the Priest and church , because if truth be told Mary and Philip blamed them both for killing Gerrard.

If the Priest had not been abusing her Son he would still be here. If the Priest had not been abusing Jonjo McNeil then Charlie might still be here on the outside world, so who else was to blame if not the Priest and Church?

All those years ago Mary thought she was taking sanctuary within the confines of what the Church could provide and placed her faith that it would keep her and her secret safe.

Then she had allowed Gerrard to become an Alter boy , had encouraged him in a way to play his part in the Church, explaining it would always be a safe haven for him a place where he could take sanctuary if he ever found himself troubled, and look what had happened to him

However, now after everything which had gone on with her family and the loss she had suffered, the realization hit her that there was NO SANCTUARY to be had !

THE END

CPSIA information can be obtained
at www.ICGtesting.com
Printed in the USA
LVOW03s0841150516

488335LV00013B/290/P